Andrew Jackson Davis

A Stellar Key to the Summer Land

Andrew Jackson Davis

A Stellar Key to the Summer Land

ISBN/EAN: 9783337372583

Printed in Europe, USA, Canada, Australia, Japan

Cover: Foto ©Andreas Hilbeck / pixelio.de

More available books at **www.hansebooks.com**

A

STELLAR KEY

TO

THE SUMMER LAND.

BY

ANDREW JACKSON DAVIS,

AUTHOR OF "NATURE'S DIVINE REVELATIONS," "HARMONIA," "ARABULA,"
AND OTHER VOLUMES ON THE "HARMONIAL PHILOSOPHY."

PART I.

ILLUSTRATED WITH DIAGRAMS AND ENGRAVINGS OF CELESTIAL
SCENERY.

BOSTON:

WILLIAM WHITE & COMPANY,

158 WASHINGTON STREET.

NEW YORK:

BANNER OF LIGHT BRANCH OFFICE, 544 BROADWAY.

1867.

AN EXPLANATORY WORD.

This volume is designed to furnish Scientific and Philosophical Evidences of the Existence of an Inhabitable Sphere or Zone among the Suns and Planets of Space. These evidences are indispensable, being adapted to all who seek a solid, rational, philosophical Foundation on which to rest their hopes of a substantial existence after death.

A. J. D.

New York,
December 15th, 1867.

CONTENTS OF PART I.

A STELLAR KEY.

CHAPTER I.

THE discovery and announcement of that wonderful and interminable relationship between the material universe and the spiritual universe—a relationship founded in the immutable laws of existence, by which things visible are bound by the ties of fertile sympathy to realms of causation invisible—could not but astonish and delight the boldest poetic imagination, and excite the opposition and ridicule of those skeptics who rely for what they term " positive knowledge," upon the industry and testimony of their five bodily senses.

The discovery of the law of Gravitation, notwithstanding its far-stretching penetrations into the profoundest secrets and fixed operations of the great Positive Mind, was not a thousandth part as important and world-lifting as was the disclosure of an inhabitable and a really inhabited belt of solid spiritualized matter in the heavens, adapted to the new bodies, and new senses, and new necessities, of men, and women, and children, who are born on this planet, and who unfail-

ingly withdraw from it through the process called
" Death."

Like thankful children, bending in reverential grati-
tude beneath the unutterable glory of the Central Sun
—the throne, so to speak, of the all-loving Mother and
omniscient Father of All—we approach the repositories
of ideas and essences, and ask for such facts and such
illustrations as can be seen and admitted by philosophers and skeptics of the most materialistic habits of
thought. We seek for data in the recognized fields
of positive knowledge, for scientific facts and recent discoveries in matter, which shall serve as stepping-stones
for the millions, whereby they can, intellectually and
rationally, gain a clear vision of spheres celestial and
heavenly.

The world-cheering discovery of the shining belt, to
which I have alluded, has arrived by degrees; coming
through the hazy glimmerings of man's intuitions from
remotest ages; stealing with beneficent mysteriousness
through the hopes of mankind ; seen like the light of a
distant taper shining through openings in thinnest
clouds; felt in the reasonings and wonderful generalizations of astronomers; beheld by the entranced poet and
by the inspired artist as a permanent *reality* beyond the
starry confines; contemplated by analogical reasoners
as a capacious Existence—adapted to, and yearned for
by the immortal mind—a world swimming somewhere
in space, where star or planet never rolled; demonstrated to the senses of spiritualists by " sounds," not
uncertain, like the voices of distant waters heard through
a landscape unknown, but *distinct* and *positive*, telling
of a home for you and for me in the solemn abysses of

space; and, lastly, looked upon by the bright eyes of independent clairvoyants, who have discerned its constitution, read its sublime mysteries, disclosed the grandeur of the planetary mechanism, described the illustrious beings who repose there in contemplation, and the thronging hosts, also, who, with human affections and infinitely diversified attractions, people that substantial and eternal sphere, not built with hands, in the bosom of the heavens.

The relationship and sympathy between the orbs and spheres of immensity—between this world of humanity and that better world of humanity arisen—are recognized naturally and inevitably by man's intuitions and reason. It comes like a gleam of glory sent into finite minds from the Central Sun; and he is unreverential to truth, not to say wicked and dogmatic, who turns away from it with contempt. "Man is immortal," is the world's affirmation. "Is it otherwise possible in the government of the Universe?" asks a writer. "Shall the material thing, inorganic, inert, impercipient, move on in this wondrous perpetuity; and shall the soul which discerns its order and tracks its career, and detects its laws and speculates on its constitution, be swept away as nothing before it? Shall unconscious matter last, while the mind, to which alone its functions are subservient, which interprets its mysteries and reads them in the signature of God, vanish like the passing wind? Shall the knowledge and the thoughts of men be handed down in endless genealogy, teaching and inspiring the soul of other times; and shall the conscious creature which called them into being be blotted ignominiously from creation? Impossible! It cannot be but that they, through the medium of whose thought we now gaze at the skies, witness elsewhere the excellence of their past toils, the triumphs of their studious meditations. Surely the Heavens which they deciphered, they behold with eyes undimmed by age, and minds yet yearning, but in a spirit of profounder adoration, to press forward toward vaster disclosures of the infinitude of God!"

Looking far into the ages past, and making the laborious march of man's history with regard to his acquisition of positive knowledge, I find accurate conceptions, more or less mixed with the reflections of superstition and the colorings of fancy, of the *realities* pertaining to a higher sphere of human existence. At first it was natural for the individual mind to be narrow in its conceptions, because its views were mainly derived from outward observations of the skies. But now, at an era when the human race is no longer in its infancy, the individual's reason can take in purer sentiments and larger conceptions, derived from discoveries of those unchangeable laws and principles which sustain and regulate the stupendous combinations of infinite harmonies. The Intuition of past generations, like the totality of the Reason of those now living, gives out no conflicting testimony on the *physical possibility* of an inhabitable sphere or zone of spiritualized matter in space, called recently the Summer Land.

It is no dream, remember, but a demonstration consummated at the lower end of Herschel's telescope, that scattered through the measureless expanse of blue ether, but in the very perfection of order and harmony, are groups of stars and systems of suns, occupying in the heavens positions which are, to the unarmed eye, covered and filled with only boundless fields of nebu- læ. Scientific astronomy, by its marvelous discoveries, has thus expanded men's minds with respect to the fir- mamental magnitudes and planetary splendors of the material universe. The cosmogonies of illimitable space are fast coming into popular education. It is now conceded, even by anthropomorphists and other unprogressive religionists, that instead of the earth being at the *center* of God's universe, and instead of the doings and omissions of its denizens being the chief concern and perpetual misery of the entire Trinity, our sun and its planets belong to the Milky Way not only, but that the Milky Way itself is merely *one* communi- ty of suns and planets of an infinitude of similar sys- tems and communities that float and sing the songs of harmony, in the celestial atmosphere of the univercœ- lum! "Where are we, after all," asks an astronomer, " but in the center of a sphere, whose circumference is 35,000 times as far from us as Sirius, and beyond whose circuit boundless infinity stretches unfathomed as ever. In our first conceptions, the distance of the earth from the sun is a quantity almost infinite. Compare it with the intervals between the fixed stars, and it becomes no quantity at all, but only an infinitesimal. Now, when the spaces between the stars are contrasted with the gulfs of dark space separating firmaments, they abso- lutely vanish below us. Can the whole firmamental creation, in its turn, be only a corner of some mightier scheme—*a mere nebula itself?* Probably *Coleridge* is not in error :—' It is not impossible that to some infi- nitely superior Being the whole universe may be as one

1*

plain—the distance between planet and planet being only as the pores in a grain of sand, and the spaces between system and system no greater than the intervals between one grain and the grain adjacent!'"

The stupendous character of the truths thus far unfolded by astronomy must act beneficially upon the human mind. But it is my impression that the resolution of the nebulæ of immensity into millions of suns, with their attendant minor systems of inhabitable planets and uninhabitable satellites, asteroids, and comets, is, notwithstanding its amazing, and engrossing, and overwhelming vastness and sublime beauty, nothing more than a look within the vestibule of the Eternal Temple! The measureless systems of stars and suns, which roll and swim and eddy and waltz about in their harmonial circles, shine upon landscapes more beautiful, and into eyes more divine than ours!

CHAPTER II.

IMMORTAL MIND LOOKING INTO THE HEAVENS.

IN accordance with the imperious law of attraction—a law which is as palpably felt and manifested in mind as in matter—the thinking powers energetically force their way through space, and find a stand-point from which they can contemplate the sublimity and reality of trans-mundane lands of human existence. The starry heavens awaken and invite the inmost, intensest love of immortality. The deep-seeing philosophical faculties of man's Reason will not, because they cannot, stop with the limitations of the five senses. The principles of nature flow into the intuitions of the reverential, free, untrammeled student. They teach him to think industriously, and to march onward and upward; and if he be conscientious, a devout lover of what is exactly true and exactly just, Nature will keep him within the legitimate sphere of logical reasoning.

The Scottish philosopher, who found true appreciation after he had entered the societies of arisen humanity in the starry heavens, Dr. Dick, when considering the possibility of a higher world of human life, says: "But there are certain general and admitted principles on which we may reason, and there are certain phenomena and indications of design exhibited in the structure of the universe, from which certain general conclusions may be deduced; beyond such generalities I

do not intend to proceed, nor to indulge in vain conjecture."

From the magnitude and harmonious arrangements
of the stellar universe, the philosopher derived conclusions, that, on the planets in space, which circle around
their parent suns, other persons like ourselves really
could and do exist. His enlarging thoughts and figures
are: "If this earth, which ranks among the smaller
globes of our system, contains such an immense number
of living bodies (30,000,000,000,000), what must be the
number of sentient and intellectual existences in all the
worlds to which we have alluded! We are assured, on
certain data, that 2,019,100,000,000 worlds may exist
within the bounds of the visible universe; and, although
no more beings should exist in each world, at an aver-
age, than on our globe, there would be the following
number of living inhabitants in these worlds, 60,573,-
000,000,000,000,000,000,000; that is, sixty quadrillions,
five hundred and seventy-three thousand trillions, a
number which transcends human conception."

"We would now ask, in the name of all that is
sacred," continues this philosopher, "whether such
magnificent manifestations of Deity ought to be considered as irrelevant in the business of religion, and
whether they ought to be thrown completely into the
shade, in the discussions which take place on religious
topics, in the assemblies of the saints. If religion consists in the intellectual apprehension of the perfections
of truth, and in the moral effects produced by such an
apprehension, shall we rest contented with a less glorious idea of God than his works are calculated to afford?
Perhaps some may be disposed to insinuate that the

views above stated are above the level of ordinary comprehensions, and founded too much on scientific considerations, to be stated in detail to a common audience. To any insinuations of this kind it may be replied, that such illustrations as those to which we have referred are more easily comprehended than many of those abstract discussions to which they are frequently accustomed; since they are definite and tangible, being derived from those objects which strike the senses and imagination."

The far-stretching powers of the human mind appear grandly in the contemplations of this mountain philosopher. How energetically did his thinking faculties grasp the fundamental idea of an open intercourse between the inhabitants of the two worlds! "Whether we may ever enjoy an intimate correspondence with beings belonging to other worlds, is a question which will frequently obtrude itself on a contemplative mind. It is evident that, in our common state, all direct intercourse with other worlds is impossible. The law of gravitation, which unites all the worlds in the universe in one grand system, separates man from his kindred spirits in other planets, and interposes an impassable barrier to his excursions to distant regions, and to his correspondence with other orders of intellectual beings. But in the present state he is only in the *infancy of his being;* he is destined to a future and eternal state of existence, where the range of his faculties and his connections with other beings will be indefinitely expanded. 'A wide and boundless prospect lies before him,' and during the revolution of interminable duration, he will, doubtless, be brought into contact and correspondence with numerous orders of kindred beings, with whom he may be permitted to associate on terms of equality and of enduring friendship. But should the laws of the physical system, and the immense distances which intervene between the several worlds, prevent such associations as I have now supposed, there may be *another* economy, superior to the physical, which may consist with the most extensive and intimate intercourse of all rational and virtuous beings. There may be a *spiritual* economy established in the universe, of which the physical structure of creation is the basis, or platform, or the introductory scene in which rational beings are trained and prepared for being members of the higher order of this celestial or intellectual economy. It appears highly probable that the first introduction of every rational creature into existence is on the scene of a *physical* economy."

Thus, naturally and philosophically, the free reason of man works at something approximating to the celestial truth of an inhabitable belt, the Summer Land, so gloriously demonstrated in this more favored age and receptive country. In one place this philosopher exclaims : " Oh, could we wing our way with the swiftness of a seraph, from sun to sun, and from world to world, until we had surveyed all the systems visible to the naked eye, which are only as a mere speck in the map of the universe—could we, at the same time, contemplate the glorious landscapes and scenes of grandeur they exhibit—could we also mingle with the pure and exalted intelligences which people those resplendent abodes, and behold their humble and ardent adorations of their Almig'ity Maker, their benign and condescending deportment toward one another—'each esteeming another better than himself'—and all united in the bonds of the purest affection, without one haughty or discordant feeling—what indignation and astonishment would seize us on our return to this obscure corner of creation."

Thus, dimly, but energetically and assuredly, a profound belief in the wondrous system of the relationship and sympathy between the terrestrial and celestial spheres of existence, burns its way deeply into the thinking powers of men's minds. A mighty and mysterious unity of plan is revealed, with boundless diversities and orderly perturbations, all moving onward together through the ever-deepening depths of infinitude, teaching the human mind reverentially to look up, contemplate, and unfold in wisdom and love.

But inasmuch as it is not the object of these chapters to recount the evidences of immortality, the reader is referred, for a full investigation of man's efforts to satisfy his mind on the subject of a future life, to the Great Harmonia, Vol. V., Part III., wherein both the inferential and the positive evidences are revealed to the thinking faculties.

CHAPTER III.

DEFINITION OF SUBJECTS UNDER CONSIDERATION.

To every intelligent, rational, existence-loving mind, the question naturally and plainly occurs : " Is there a substantial world for human beings to live in after death ?"

Hope and faith give light and peace to minds of fine sentiments and intuitive sensibilities. But to the hard-headed and sensuous positive thinker, the light of "hope" is valued as only an *ignis fatuus*, and the peace of " faith " as the delusive dream of weak and idle minds. · Beautiful as is faith, and comforting as is hope, to those to whom these internal evidences of immortality are sufficient, they have no weight with those who look upon the universe as a mechanism developed by no intelligence outside of the inherent principles of life and motion. It is to meet the needs of this class, especially, that the evidences will be unfolded and weighed under several distinct heads :—

First. The *Possibility* of Summer Land in the heavens ;

Second. Its *Probability* in the structure of the Universe ;

Third. Its *Certainty*, as demonstrated by the arrangement and order of the Stars ;

Fourth. Its *Formation*, in the shape of a stratified belt of matter ;

FIFTH. Its *Constitution* of materials drawn from the inhabited planets;

SIXTH. Its *Location* among the systems and constellations in the sky.

Under the impression that, with the positive philosophers of our day, all clairvoyant testimony would be invalid, I am constrained, in order to prosecute the design of this work, to proceed wholly from an inductive stand-point. There is an inherent force in truth, however, which carries it straight and triumphantly into man's understanding, if it is so fortunate as to be presented free from the cumbrous and imposing superstitions and embarrassing atheistic logic of the times. The august and harmonious temple of the universe, if entered by man with a reverential love of truth in his heart, is sure, though slowly, to open mansion after mansion, and glory after glory, to the welcomed visitor.

All minds sincerely desirous of true knowledge, can seek and find it in those harvest-fields of the celestial realm, which stretch away, and are lost to the imagination, but not to the logical reason, beyond suns and stars in the boundless blue. And it is to aid such minds in their faithful searchings, that these chapters are now written and submitted.

CHAPTER IV.

THE POSSIBILITY OF THE SPIRITUAL ZONE.

In this chapter it is proposed to approach the subject from the outermost rim of the wheel of inductive reasoning. The subject under investigation is embodied in the following affirmation : THERE IS AN INHABITABLE ZONE, OR A CIRCULAR BELT OF REFINED AND STRATIFIED MATTER IN THE HEAVENS WHICH RECENTLY HAS BEEN DENOMINATED " THE SUMMER LAND." The possibility of the existence of this material belt in the Stellar Universe is to be considered, in this part of our work, as though there was no such a power as "clairvoyance," and no such manifestations as "spiritual." All evidences, therefore, however irresistible and sacred to those who believe in these realities, are, in this stage of our inquiry, to be "ruled out," as not valid to the positivists and inductive reasoners who, we are now supposing, compose the honorable assembly of rigid investigators before us.

The name of "Man" was, I think, derived from certain Greek roots which signify "to spring up," "to look up," or to grow and rise upward. Therefore many ages ago the Greeks, inspired by the genius of truth, made the discovery that *man* is organized for progression, which is the "real" meaning of the word "Man." Accordingly, if men would be *true* men, they must, in the language of Kepler, "think the thoughts of God after him." Such thinking, which is the grandest attainment of education, the most divine and ennobling consummation of deep and methodical reasoning, is possible only to those who think and reason in harmony with the facts of Science and the fixed principles of Nature.

Superficial high-mindedness, or the positiveness of ignorance and the pride of knowledge, seal the soul to the influx of God's Spirit and Wisdom. A heart that can love truth, as fast as the honest reason discerns it, and a conscience that will firmly and steadily steer life's barque in harmony with such feeling and such conviction, are vast riches to their possessor. The overarching heavens come very near, in their gracious light and serene beauty, to the mind and heart that is attuned to their unchangeable ways. Brightness, penetration, celerity, calmness, and comprehensiveness are some of the characteristics of the Stellar Universe. " To think the thoughts of God after him," would be, in astronomy, thinking in accordance with the *interior* forces and the harmonious manifestations thereof in the visible universe. Dull minds sleep behind dull senses; but star-eyed persons possess minds shining full of heavenly splendors.

But it is not possible, for manifold causes of a purely extrinsic character, that all minds should come in immediate rapport with the fundamental or primitive founts of knowledge. Hence, in the words of a modern scholar: " We must try to get the best of Greece and of Rome, by rapid study of the genius of the languages, and by grasping the wealth of the literatures; and what we have no time to get by minute study of the originals, we must seek by lectures of erudite scholars, and by reading. In our want of time to seek knowledge in all the old fields, it is a consolation to know that the treasures of the ancient languages float down the stream of time, and are lodged in the new literatures. Goethe and Lessing, in Germany, were almost as much Greeks as if they had lived with Pericles at Athens. Next to having read all of Cicero, is to read Forsyth's Life of Cicero; or all of Epictetus, is to be familiar with Higginson's translation; or all of Antoninus, is to know Long's paraphrase. . . . A great change has come; the world has moved forward; the nations have come closer together; modern languages have become necessary to the intelligent citizen for travel, trade, and acquaintance with the world's affairs and thoughts.

"And then, how wonderful the rise and progress of science in these last fifty years. Astronomy stood almost alone as a science in the last century. Chemistry was breaking out of its chrysalis, the old Alchemy, and crude thoughts of cosmogony, and of the plants and animals, made a chaos of knowledge, void and formless. And now think for one moment of all these sciences that have presented such various and interesting fields of inquiry and thought; each one so vastly enlarging and enriching our life, and each opening a new pathway to the mysterious agencies of God's creation and providence."

We ask the world's thinkers and scholars to step out of the old into the "new pathway" that leads to the "mysterious agencies of God's creation and providence." But science can know nothing of "the mysterious agencies of God." What it knows, it knows; all the rest is speculation. But by speculations and calculations based upon what science knows, a world of knowledge has been acquired in astronomy, in chemistry, in geology, &c. Why, upon the same principles of inductive reasoning and inferential conjecture, may not greater results be obtained in higher departments of the universe? Astronomers, chemists, geologists, ethnologists, and other physicists, have obtained some of their best results by following perturbations, slight effects, hints, and signs, and the world does not denounce these scientists as dreamers and visionaries in the airy realms of hypotheses; on the contrary, they are justly regarded and gratefully remembered as well-disciplined mathematicians, as accurate thinkers, as men of profoundest erudition, and as benefactors of mankind.

The *possibility* of the existence of the stratified Zone in the heavens, may be considered with reference to the structures and locations of the different solar systems in space. Of course a thing is often esteemed as *possible*, which is neither certain nor even probable; in fact, logically, both the improbability and the uncertainty of a matter is implied in its "possibility." It is possible that every person on earth may, within one year, believe in the existence of the stratified Zone; but it is not remotely probable, and falls infinitely short of a certainty. When a thing or an event does not contradict the known laws of the possible, then men say, "it *may* be so," or, "it may exist," or, "it may happen;" but, in so saying, the *improbabilities* and the *uncertainties* are understood as implied by the primary admission. There is a *possibility* that a shower of falling meteors may occur at ten o'clock this night, or that a great earthquake will sink the entire western

continent day after to-morrow ; but there is no certainty
of it, and, judging from the usual course of nature,
there is not even "the most distant probability" that
any such earthquake will ever happen on this planet. On
the other hand, it is logical to say, positively, that some
things and events are absolutely "impossible." Probabilities and certainties are—in such decisions and positive declarations of the self-evident consciousness—left
entirely out of the mind. For example, because Mount
Everest, of the Himalaya range, is twenty-nine thousand
feet high, it is not possible for every other mountain in
the world to report an equal elevation. Nor is it possible for mountains to exist without valleys between
them, or that seas and oceans can exist without depres-
sions in the earth's surface *lower* than the arable and
populated lands. It is not possible for two halves to
be less or more than the whole. It is not possible that
twice five should be either nine or eleven.

And so men reason about some things and events
that are intrinsically and self-evidently *impossible*, and
concerning other things and events that are intrinsically
and self-evidently *possible*, while probabilities and certainties are infinitely more remote from the admissions
of the logical intellect.

CHAPTER V.

THE ZONE IS POSSIBLE IN THE VERY NATURE OF THINGS.

LOOKING into the sky, and carefully examining the form of the planets in the stellar sphere, you remark, first of all, that the *shape* of sun and moon and stars is round. Therefore, the heavenly bodies are properly called "globes," while the word "planet" signifies to stray, to wander, or "the traveler."

The Chaldeans, as well as other Oriental nations, were profound students of the stars. They observed, naturally enough, just as you do, unaided by telescopes, and without using astro-mathematics, the existence of bright spherical bodies, which, because they have never been known to alter their grand and imposing configurations and relative positions, are called "fixed stars." These stars, according to the ancients, were unalterably fixed in the firmament, or firm-built vault, which, they thought, revolved upon its axis, an immeasurable hollow sphere rolling diurnally around the earth, which was by them supposed to be an immovable flat and boundless stretch of land and water.

The sphere of the fixed stars—each the throne of some unintelligible and lawless deity or demon—by revolving around the motionless earth, produced the effects of rising and setting among all the heavenly bodies. It is not strange that the sun was by the ancients supposed to be the effulgent seat of the master-god, whose almighty fiat

THE GREAT CENTRAL SUN.

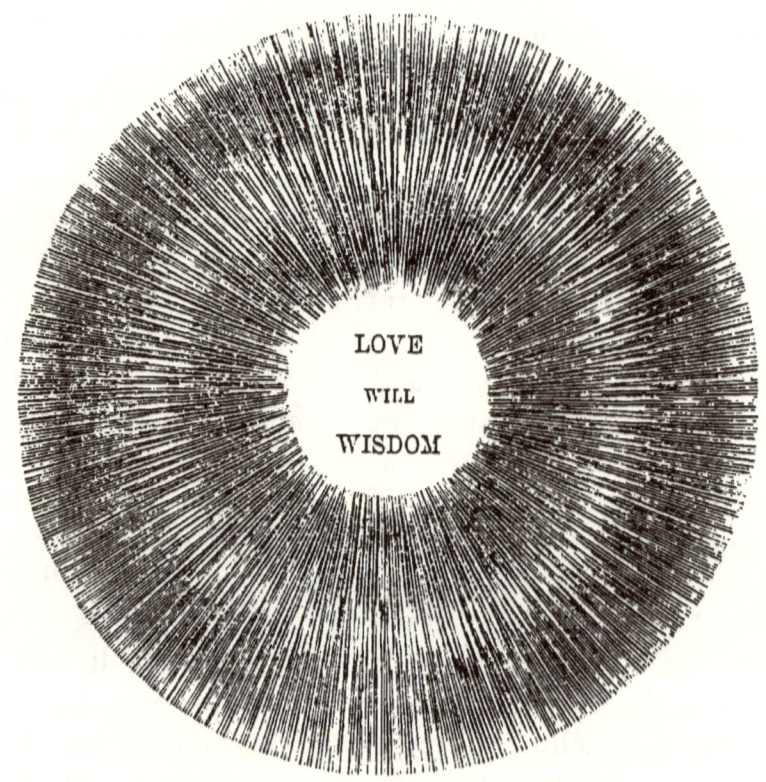

LOVE

WILL

WISDOM

SUN OF THE INTERIOR UNIVERSE.

The great original, ever-existing, omniscient, omnipotent, and omni-present productive power—the Soul of all existences—is throned in a central sphere, the circumference of which is the boundless universe, and around which solar, sidereal, and stellar systems revolve, in silent, majestic sublimity and harmony! This power is what mankind call Deity, whose attributes are love and wisdom, corresponding with the principles of male and female, positive and negative, sustaining and creative.

caused all the marvelous movements among the heavenly bodies, unfolded the spangling panorama of the skies, emitted thunder and lightning, wheeled the blazing comet, sent meteoric or shooting stars, and filled the solitudes of immensity with fearful catastrophes; neither is it strange that the human race, in its infancy, should have, out of appearance of the heavenly bodies, slowly elaborated a mythological theology, an astrological system of identifying the birth, life, fortunes, and misfortunes of individuals with the wills and good or evil conjunctions of conflicting divinities, supposed to inhabit the different stars in the revolving sphere.

The progression of astronomical science has demonstrated many truths, and exposed many errors, accumulated and held sacred by the ancients. The roundness of the solar bodies has been settled by science. But the rotating spheres or circles of fixed stars, and the imposing illusion that the heavens are in the shape of a vault, have been perfectly removed by the hand of astronomical discovery. The Ptolemaic system, which admitted the notion of an indefinite number of starry rings or rotating circles, has not been wholly set aside, except in so far as the complete celestial mechanism is concerned; for do we not read in modern astronomy of the *paths* of the comets, of the *orbits* of the planets, and of the *track* of the sun, and all the stellar family from west to east, toward some more interior center or system in the solemn depths of infinitudes? Ptolemy and Hipparchus of Alexandria, during the reigns of Adrian and Antonine at Rome, made astronomy a considerable degree more scientific and reliable; although the groupings and calculations of the planets were based upon the

2

cumbersome machinery of diversal circles, in which the sun, moon, and stars were supposed to be fixed, like so many bright bodies fastened firmly to a multitude of narrow wheels of immense diameter. This supposition, however, was accepted and urged more by those less talented men who succeeded Ptolemy, and who, without learning, advocated and degraded his more perfect system.

What you are now asked to observe, is, first, the spherical form or *roundness* of the heavenly bodies; and, second, the circular orbit, or *wheel-like* path, in which they all uniformly revolve. The appearance of the sun to the natural eye is that of an immense globe of fire! It is by astronomers said to contain more than seven hundred times as much matter as all the planets in our system; some, by careful computation, declare that the sun is one million and four hundred thousand times greater in magnitude than the earth. And yet this earth is so very large, so vast in extent, that ethnologists and antiquarians are still searching for races and relics in regions not explored by civilized man.

The sun is round, remember, and that it is rolling in a vast circular path through the dizzy abysses of space; so also do all the planets move and roll in the same direction, from west to east, around the all-controlling sun; and, what is still more remarkable, in all this sublime scene of starry harmony and supernal splendor, is, that all the planets perform their diurnal and annual revolutions on nearly the same plane.

Whilst the essential characteristics of all planetary motions, like the form and shape of the planets themselves, are circularity and roundness, it should be borne in mind that the cometary and meteoric bodies, which

THE SUN OF OUR SYSTEM.

The radiant atmosphere of our Sun pervades the whole family of stars, moons, asteroids, comets, meteoric belts, and, like a fountain, feeds all the streams of cosmical matter belonging to our solar system. Science speculatively teaches that the body of the sun was once as large as the orbit of the outermost planet.

are nothing but the bodies of cosmical space, do not strictly obey the established order and dignity of their elders and progenitors. These youngsters in the family of stars wander up and down, here and there, in and out, now up-stairs and now below in the basement of the temple—apparently acknowledging no allegiance to any of the unchangeable ways of the steady-going citizens of the skies—but run wild in all quarters of the heavens; moving in parabolas, in eccentrically extended ellipses; sometimes darting along in the direction of the sun and planets; and at other times twisting in their orbits with a retrograde motion, but generally at right angles with the plane of the earth's orbit, and never out of harmony with the whole. It is, undoubtedly, a sufficient apology for the conduct of these baby-bodies of space, these free-going offspring of suns and planets, to remember that they are yet *young*. They conduct themselves naturally, beautifully, and consistently, when their juvenility is duly considered.

Some venerable and illustrious stars, like comets and the smaller bodies, are irregular in their motions; yet all in perfect harmony with the stellar " music of the spheres." These irregular motions are often backward, forming a sort of epicycloidal curve, or in the line of the star's orbit. But no one star or comet turns or twists

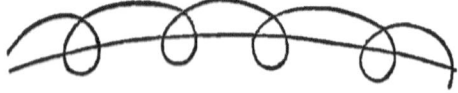

so frequently as the cut represents, which only illustrates the loops that occur; but these loopings and slight retrograde motions are merely *breathing* spells in the lungs of the great system.

But it is in the heart and sphere of the sun, in the life of the fixed stars, and in the interior constitution of the whole stupendous stellar universe, that we are to look for the inner causes and perfect principles of all planetary organizations.

What are those causes and principles? What is that fundamental law which is manifested so plainly in the *shape* and *revolution* of these heavenly bodies? Suppose that the sun, which contains more than seven hundred times as much matter as all the planets put together, should be rolled out into a broad band, like a wide ribbon drawn from the spool, what do you imagine would be the natural tendency of the matter? The first tendency would be to obey its centripetal motion, its own self-chemical attractions, and return instantly to its original globular form and condition; whilst the second tendency would be, to flow out like an interminable river through infinitude, in obedience to its centrifugal motion, and in accordance with the circular revolution it has made, together with all the planets, for an eternity of ages.

The sun's matter, thus drawn out into an unbroken elastic luminous fluid, of the consistence of molten lead or iron, would form a zone of resplendent and vivifying beauty surrounding the whole heavens, totally invisible to the unaided eye, and almost too attenuated for detection by the most powerful telescope, and yet in that rotating solar belt there would be one million and four hundred thousand times more matter than is contained in the earth's constitution!

If this river of inter-cohesive sun-matter should in time be reduced in temperature, by passing through the

resisting interstellar atmosphere, one of two events would
transpire; either the surface of the belt would become
solid like the earth's surface, or the power of cohesion
would be lost, and the zone broken into countless separate masses of nebulous matter, forming a boundless
field of luminous meteors, or cometoids, and filling the
whole solar system with material for periodical storms
of chaotic cosmical vapors—falling within the earth's
atmosphere and the intervals between the planets like
a rain of fire-mist and of burning stars. Scientifically
speaking, the former event is not supposable, because
the solar matter is too gross, and drops too low in the
scale of gravitation, to maintain a continuous stratified
surface ; and hence, following the volcanic law, the dis-
ruption and formation of sporadic masses, meteorites,
and cometary bodies in space, would be the legitimate
and scientific event.

But now—as to the *possibility!* It is not going beyond the sphere of facts, obtained by telescopic observation, to suppose the organization of a *zone* in the
heavens. We have seen the working of the principle
of globe-building, and that all planetary bodies, either
spheroidal or perfectly round, move through the
heavens in circular paths. There can be no violation
of this law in higher conditions and finer organizations
of matter. Hence, is it not *possible* in the nature of
things that a Zone of stratified substance, luminous and
inter-cohesive and circular, may exist ? If you can see
the Zone, as a *possibility* in the organization of the
universe, then you are prepared to take another step in
this investigation.

CHAPTER VI.

THE SPIRITUAL ZONE VIEWED AS A PROBABILITY.

ANY THING that is *probable* comes nearer to human credence. A possibility is exceedingly remote and obscure; whilst a probability is at hand—something within the mind's reach. The question of the probability of a Summer Land Zone in the heavens can be considered with more logical success, I think, after we have enlarged our thoughts and enriched our conceptions, by contemplating the wondrous symmetry and arraying magnitude of our solar system.

Prof. Nichol, of the University of Glasgow, borrowed from Sir John Herschel, a thought-enlarging illustration to this effect: Conceive the sun represented by a globe two feet in diameter; at eighty-two feet distance put down a *grain of mustard-seed*, and you have the size and place of the planet MERCURY, that bright silvery point which is generally enveloped in the solar rays; at the distance of one hundred and forty-two feet lay down a *pea*, and it will be the similitude of VENUS, our dazzling evening and morning star. Two hundred and fifteen feet from the central globe, place another *pea*, only imperceptibly larger—that is Man's WORLD—(once the center of the Universe !)—the theater of our terrestrial destinies — the birthplace of most of our thoughts! MARS is smaller still—a good *pin's head* being his proper representative, at the distance of three

THE ISLAND UNIVERSE.

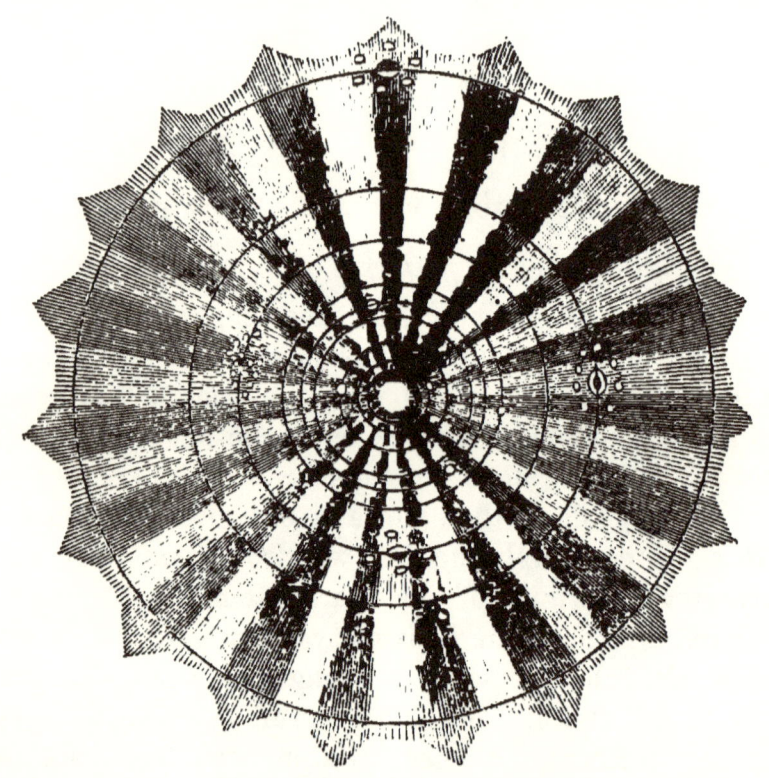

OUTLINE VIEW OF OUR SOLAR SYSTEM.

The expression "Island Universe" was suggested by the immense distance of the fixed stars from our Sun and Planets; giving the impression that our Solar System occupies an isolated position in the boundless ocean of space. See a diagram on another page.

hundred and twenty-seven feet : the small planets seem
. as the least possible *grains of sand*, about five hundred
feet from the sun ; JUPITER as a middle-sized *orange*,
distant about a quarter of a mile ; SATURN with his ring
a *lesser orange*, at the remoteness of two-fifths of amile ;
and the far URANUS dwindles into a *cherry*, moving in
a circle three-quarters of a mile in radius.   Such is the
system of which our puny earth was once accounted the
chief constituent,—a system whose real or absolute
dimensions are stupendous, as may be gathered from the
size of the SUN himself—the glorious globe around
which these orbs obediently circle ; which has a diameter
nearly four times larger than the immense interval
which separates the MOON from the EARTH.   Compare
this mighty diameter, or the space of nine hundred
thousand miles, with the assumed diameter of two feet ;
and the proportion will tell by how many times the
supposititious orbit of Uranus should be enlarged ! The
dimensions of the system surpass all effort to conceive
or embody them ; and yet a wider knowledge of the
Universe shows that they belong only to our first or
smallest order of INFINITIES.

Prof. Kirkwood, of the Washington and Jefferson
College, speaking of our solar system, says : "NEPTUNE
is the most remote known member of the system ; its
distance being nearly three thousand millions of miles.
It is somewhat larger than Uranus ; has certainly one
satellite, and probably several more.   Its period is
about one hundred and sixty-five years.   A cannon-
ball flying at the rate of five hundred miles per hour
would not reach the orbit of Neptune from the sun in
less than six hundred and eighty years.   It is proper to
2*

remark, however, that all representations of the solar system by maps and planetariums must give an exceedingly erroneous view either of the magnitudes or distances of its various members. If the earth, for instance, be denoted by a ball half an inch in diameter, the diameter of the sun, according to the same scale (sixteen thousand miles to the inch), will be between four and five feet; that of the earth's orbit, about one thousand feet; while that of Neptune's orbit will be nearly six miles. To give an accurate representation of the solar system at a single view is therefore plainly impracticable."

The vast family of planets rotate harmoniously on their own axes, each in the performance of its own individual functions and duties, and they also all revolve as harmoniously around the sun, thus causing the regular succession of days and nights on each planet, and the regular coming and going of the four beautiful and indispensable seasons. But how " various are the absolute durations of these important periods in the different bodies !" The most brilliant imagination can scarcely embrace the wonderful differences here suggested. " How, for instance," asks an astronomer, "can that contrast be pictured, which subsists between the two extreme bodies of our system, URANUS and MERCURY — the one hurrying through its restless cycle of seasons in three months, and the other spending on the same relative change eighty-four terrestrial years? A tree in Mercury—if such there be—would gather around its pith or axis three hundred and thirty-six of those well-known circular layers, in a time during which the sluggish vegetation of Uranus would only have deposited one; and a full and burning lifetime, made up of rapid sparkling joys and acute sorrows, would, in so close neighborhood of the Sun, be compressed within a space hardly adequate on earth to lead youth to its meridian—while at that outer confine a slow pulse and drowsy blood might sustain for centuries a slumbering and emotionless existence! The question is further complicated if we refer to the rapid succession of day and night in the remote planets; perhaps modifying, by the activity it excites, the comparative torpidity due to the length of the year. We can form no notion of the physiological consequences due to a recurrence of day and night within the brief period of nine or ten hours."

In another place the same author says: " We know that long progress is essential to our planet's destiny; and surely it is not alone amid the planetary scheme—not alone does it undergo the apparently necessary fate of all beings subject to the empire of time and space. Granting that every planet has a life of its own—an interior and self-comprehended principle, by which it is led through mighty developments, the question recurs, whether there is unity or connection among these principles—whether the orbs proceed and pass into new forms, according to similar or related laws—whether, in short, the system has one central governing principle, a common life running through the whole, explaining its contrarieties, warming and animating them all, as man's life circulates with his blood? To a question so bold, we cannot here give an answer. Other objects must first be surveyed, especially the *seat* of the power, which, if it exists, is necessarily the Sun.

"But is LIFE in all these planets? Through all possible schemes, through all conditions of a globe's evolving organization, is what we call LIFE an inseparable or essential concomitant? Life, visible or invisible—*i. e.*, the sentient and intelligent principle—nay, even, *progressive* life, a growing and evolving Reason—is doubtless an essential element of the universe; perhaps the very highest development of any imaginable energy; such Life may be diffused without limit, may assume forms and be connected with bodies or centers, of which man has obtained hitherto only the most confined idea; but to the fulfilling and realizing of this aim, is it necessary that small, sentient, self-contained organisms —worshiping, with few dissents, their peculiar IDOLS of the tribe, den, forum and theater—shall move over the surface of each planet? Beautiful the carpeting which covers vast portions of the earth, a carpeting on which sorrow often treads, but chiefly joy—now bounding in youth, now placid in manhood, and meditative in age—but that is not universal! I reflect on history— on the fact that such life seems among the incidents, the befalling things of our globe's mysterious destiny; and my mind recurs to solitudes—to its still existing deserts, which even the patient camel does not enter without a shudder; to valleys with giant sides, where the unsightly Cretin, and the frequent glare of idiocy, speak of formations inhospitable to man. Sovereign Blanc! Neither is thy bare forehead, which not even a lichen has ever stained, an outcast from the great scheme of things—uncomprehended, unwarmed by the world's indwelling Soul!"

CHAPTER VII.

EVIDENCES OF ZONE-FORMATIONS IN THE HEAVENS.

In this department of the subject we are impression-
ally admonished to take the testimony of astronomers,
and of known scientists in other regions of inquiry ; so
that the physical or sensuous side of our " spiritual "
question may be amply represented, and all the external
evidences adduced, for the gratification and benefit of
inductive reasoners in general. In future chapters the
deductive or more spiritual evidences and philosophical
arguments will appear ; so that, from an innumerable
multitude of facts suggested and principles explained,
the *certainty* of the celestial Zone may be established ;
or, at least, be deemed by the truly scientific a question
worthy of the strictest and most patient investigation.
The illustrious Shelley, in one of his comprehensive
celestial visions, saw beyond the sweep of Lord Rosse's
immense telescope :

> " Earth's distant orb appears
> The smallest orb that twinkles in the heavens ;
> Whilst round the chariot's way
> Innumerable systems rolled,
> And countless spheres diffused
> An ever-varying glory."

The probability of the Summer Land Zone, as a
material *reality* in the Structure and sublime Economy

of the heavens, will dawn first upon that mind which rationally understands the causative principles *within* the belt-building manifestations of cosmical matter. On this ring-forming tendency of all atoms in space, let us take the testimony of astronomers.

And first let us hear from an astronomical investigator, whose mathematical paper on the Nebular Hypotheses, appeared in the "American Journal of Science and Arts" (Vol. XXXVIII. Nov., 1864), and which has been pronounced as adding something "new" by several eminent astronomers. The entire treatise should be consecutively read, in justice to the argument and its author, but for the present purpose a few extracts will suffice.

The Original Condition of Matter.—Geology has revealed the fact that it took immense ages of time to form the earth, and fit it for the habitation of man. The same science also points somewhat definitely to a time when the earth was in a highly heated condition. Mathematical science, applied to the problem of the earth's conformation, teaches us that the earth has that form—the asperities of its surface not considered —which it ought to have if it were in a fluid state when it assumed its present form. These facts—to which we might add the condition of Saturn's rings— seem to teach that the earth, and in short the whole *Solar System*, were once in an aëriform state. An additional argument in favor of this view, is derived from the physical constitution of *Comets*.

The Operations of Heat.—Philosophers, in their investigations, have arrived at this general conclusion respecting the operation of heat, namely, that mechanical action develops it, and the greater the action the greater the heat; and that as soon as heat becomes sensible, it tends to change the condition of bodies. This, then, reduces the cause of the primitive gaseous state of the stellar and planetary worlds to mechanical action. As the mechanical action becomes less and less, the operations of heat become less and less potent.

Motions of different Bodies.—Around the different centers, matter would accumulate and condense, and these nuclei, so formed, would revolve around their common center of gravity. As soon as a rotary motion had commenced, centrifugal forces would begin to act; and as the process of cooling continued, the attraction of gravitation would have a greater control (for the tendency of heat is to expand all bodies, and thus to operate against the attraction of cohesion, and also of gravitation in the case which we are considering), and thus the mass would be condensed, and the rotatory motion thereby increased. Each nucleus would itself be in a condition very similar to that which at first existed in the original great fluid mass.

Origin of the Spherical Zone.—A fluid mass which does not rotate on an axis must ultimately become spherical in form, whatever be the law of attraction. But if it have a rotatory motion, it can never become a sphere, although it may approximate to one in form. A fluid body which rotates on an axis will be swelled out at the equator; that is, the particles of matter will be thrown from the axis of rotation, and there will consequently be a depression about the poles.

In the case of a homogeneous spheroid there are, with a slow rotation, two forms of equilibrium, one of which is an oblate spheroid of *small* ellipticity, and the other is an oblate spheroid of *great* ellipticity.

Plane of the Zone-Formations.—The primitive solar spheroid could have only approximated to a symmetrical form, and to a symmetrical disposition of its materials, especially in the outer parts. If it were so constituted, it is difficult to see how it could separate into rings of much width; but the materials being somewhat heterogeneously distributed, a ring of considerable width might be thrown off, or rather abandoned.

The *invariable plane* of the solar system must be the invariable plane of the primitive solar spheroid, and that must have coincided approximately with the plane of the equator. The first planetary ring abandoned would have an inclination to the plane of the equator nearly the same as that of the principal plane; and thus the outermost planet of the solar system should move in an orbit whose inclination is nearly the same as that of the principal plane of the solar system. By making as exact a determination as possible, M. Lespiault has found the inclination of the invariable plane to be 1° 41'. The inclination of the orbit of Neptune is 1° 46" 59", the correspondence of these two numbers is rather remarkable.

The Existence and Location of Zones.—Prof. Peirce, of Harvard University, in his investigation of the problem of the stability of the motions of Saturn's rings, arrived at the remarkable conclusion that the dynamical equilibrium of the rings is preserved by the sustaining effect of satellites in the very act of perturbation. He then makes the remark, that the only place in the Solar System, among the primary planets, where we could, from the above conclusions, expect a permanent ring, is just within the powerful masses of Jupiter and Saturn.

A Zone Existing for Innumerbble Ages.—Basing our reasoning on the preceding results, we are led to the conclusion that under certain conditions—such as probably exist within the orbits of Jupiter and Saturn in the Solar System—the abandoned fluid ring may preserve its form for *immense ages*, and thus have time to cool down somewhat and approximate to the condition of an incompressible fluid. . . . Under certain conditions—such as Prof. Peirce has found to exist in the System of Saturn—a ring, or rings, might remain entire.

Revolutions of the Cosmical Ether.—If there exists a cosmical ether (as is at present generally admitted), in order that it may remain spread throughout universal space, it is only necessary for it to possess an elasticity so great that the action of luminous bodies is sufficient to produce a mechanical action in it that will enable it to maintain its temperature and fluid condition under all circumstances. This cosmical ether being material in its nature, it would necessarily partake of the motion of those bodies with which it remains in contact for immense ages of time. In the Solar System, the motion of the ether around the sun would be in the general direction of all the planets.

Harmony and Correspondence throughout the Universe.—Mr. Nasmyth, in the "Annual of Scientific Discovery," for 1857, says: Every well-trained philosophical judgment is accustomed to observe illustrations of the most sublime phenomena of creation in the most minute and familiar operations of the Creator's laws, one of the most characteristic features of which consists in the absolute and wonderful integrity maintained in their action, whatsoever be the range as to magnitude or distance of the objects on which they operate. For instance, the minute particles of dew which whiten the grass-blade in early morn, are, in all probability, molded into spheres by the identical law which gives to the mighty sun its globular form. It is remarkable of physical laws, that we see them operating on every kind of scale as to magnitude, with the same regularity and perseverance. . . Two eddies in a stream fall into a mutual revolution at the distance of a couple of inches, through the same cause that makes a pair of suns link in mutual revolution at the distance of millions of miles. There is, we might say, a sublime simplicity in this indifference of the grand regulations to the vastness or the minuteness of the field of their operations. We thus may learn, from the minuter operations of nature, of those grand revolutions which we have reason to conclude have taken place in past ages of duration.

Saturn's Belts an Illustration.—The rings of Saturn offer a living example of the primitive secondary rings. They open to us, in a measure, the nature and constitution of the primitive rings, both the primary and secondary.*

Prof. Kirkwood, in his Treatise on Meteoric Astronomy, says that the most probable opinion, based on the

---

* These extracts from Prof. Trowbridge indicate the information and speculations extant among scientific men on the formation and existence of zones, or rings of cosmical matter.

researches of astronomers, is, that Saturn's rings "consist of streams or clouds of meteoric asteroids. The zodiacal light, and the zone of small planets between Mars and Jupiter, appear to constitute analogous *primary* rings. In the latter, however, a large proportion of the primitive matter seems to have collected in distinct, segregated masses."

The same author, speaking of the asteroidal ring between Mars and Jupiter (which no man's unaided physical eyes can see), says: " The mean distances of the minor planets between Mars and Jupiter vary from 2.20 to 3.49. The breadth of the zone is therefore 20,000,000 miles *greater than the distance of the earth from the sun;* greater even than the entire interval between the orbits of Mercury and Mars. Moreover, the *perihelion* distance of some members of the group exceeds the *aphelion* distance of others by a quantity equal to the whole interval between the orbits of Mars and the earth."

Although the reader may never have investigated either of the points developed by the astronomers; yet now, since they testify to the existence of immense zones of matter, and that these zones not only continue unbroken for countless ages, but *revolve* like the planets, each on its own gravitational center or mathematical axis, are you not prepared to admit both the possibility and the *probability of a more interior reality?* This scientific external testimony naturally lays a foundation in the logical judgment for confidence in the existence of an inner universe of far exceeding beauty and glory. Although at present neither intellectually nor telescopically seen, but being not less within the domain of the rational faculties, yet the honest mind, it seems to me, cannot but give due weight to facts and principles of a more interior nature, of which these planetary formations and revolutions are merely the physical manifestations.

CHAPTER VIII.

THE SCIENTIFIC CERTAINTY OF THE SPIRITUAL ZONE.

IT has been asserted that Spiritualists, as a class, do not read carefully and investigate thoroughly; that they are superficial, shallow-minded, and credulous, believing great things upon little evidence, &c. ; but it yet remains to be determined *who* are the real embodiments of superficiality, shallowness, and feeble-minded credulity.

In considering the certainty of the Summer Land, as a stratified and inhabitable Zone in the bosom of the Stellar Universe, it becomes necessary to change the stand-point of the positive philosopher. He has stood without the temple, contemplating the phenomenal display of dynamic forces and spiritual agencies, which become visible to the eyes of reason when the philosopher explores the inner departments of the Divine Administration. In these illustrious days of enlarged and independent research, when even the great Newtonian doctrine of gravitation or central attraction has been well-nigh eclipsed by the discovery of opposite powers, or magnetic and electrical polarities within and throughout all matter,—it becomes the true philosopher to turn from the superficial and phenomenal realm of display, to turn from visible facts to the examination of the causes and principles behind them, and then to ponder well the far-reaching and fruitful lessons they legitiinately impart. Truly has it been remarked that, isolated, every thing is a mystery. All that we know depends on the connection of things one with another; and it is only by contemplating creation *as a whole* that we can attain true conceptions of its parts. This is indeed the highest exercise of the intellect, and that which more than aught else tends to develop and expand it. Even the dreamy eyes of Tennyson recognized the truth, that

"Through the ages one increasing purpose runs,
And the thoughts of men are widen'd with the process of the sun."

The mental condition of brightness, of calmness, of impartiality, which is alone adapted to the pursuit and discovery of truth, was forcibly put by Prof. Wilkinson, of London, Eng., in the introduction to one of his admirable books:—

"Incredulity of a fact, I take it, is that widespread weakness of the human mind, which is observed in men who have perfected their opinions, and have no room for learning any thing more. A new fact to them is just one above the number that is convenient or necessary for them, and had they the power of creating, or of preventing creation, the inconvenient fact should not have existed. Indeed, if admitted into their completed system, 'the little stranger' would destroy it altogether, by acting as a chemical solvent of the fabric !

"But this is not the mode of the searcher after truth; and in determining the important question which it is intended to submit for consideration, I would rather forget much that I have been taught, or find it all unsound, than I would reject one single circumstance which I know and recognize as a truth. In all the questions that can by possibility be mooted, whether philosophical or otherwise, that theory is alone admissible which will explain all the attendant phenomena and observed facts, and which is, moreover, consistent with the nature of man, and the world of matter and of mind with which he is connected.

"How true it is, that 'there are more things in heaven and earth than are dreamt of in our *philosophy*,' and yet how seldom is this great truth remembered at the right time! Although natural facts, being based, as they are, upon, and the products of Divine laws, never change, how long it is before they are recognized and adapted into our little self-formed systems; and with what throes and agonies have their acknowledgments invariably been attended! How much easier to say, 'Impossible!' and to reject the fact, than to have to reconstruct a new theory which shall embrace it, and in which it can find its home! Disbelieve, therefore, after inquiry, if you see cause, but do not begin with disbelief."

What we now ask is, that you be as truly philosophical as you have been sensuously scientific, and thus honestly examine interior causes, and weigh dynamic principles, just as you have observed effects, and reasoned from one set of appearances to another set of appearances. The profoundly philosophic Swedenborg, whose inductive reasonings shine effulgently even through the mazes of his multitudinous spiritual experiences, in his *Arcana Celestia*, 5084, says: "It is a fallacy of sense merely natural, that there are simple substances, which are monads and atoms, for whatever is within the external sensual, this the natural man believes, that it is such a thing or nothing. It is a fallacy of sense merely natural, that all things are of nature and from nature, and that indeed in purer or interior nature there is something which is not apprehended; but if it be said, that within or above nature there is the spiritual and celestial, this is rejected, and it is believed that unless it be natural, it is nothing. It is a fallacy of sense, that the body alone lives, and that its life perishes when it dies; the sensual does not at all apprehend that the internal man is in single things of the external, and that the internal man is within nature in the spiritual world: hence neither does he believe, because he does not apprehend, that he shall live after death, unless he be again clothed with a body. Hence there is a fallacy of sense, that man can no more live after death than the beasts, by reason that these also have a life in many respects similar to the life of man, only that man is a more perfect animal. The sensual does not apprehend, that is, the man who thinks and concludes from the sensual, that man is above the beasts and has a superior life in this, because he can think, not only concerning the causes of things, but also concerning the Divine, and by faith and love be conjoined with the Divine, and also receive influx thence, and appropriate it to himself, so that in man, because there is given a reciprocal, there is given reception, which is nowise the case with the beasts. It is a fallacy thence, that the living principle itself with man, which is called the soul, is only something ethereal, or flamy, which is dissipated when man dies; and that it resides either in the heart, or in the brain, or in some part thereof, and that hence it rules the body as a machine; that the internal man is in single things of the external, that the eye does not see from itself but from that internal man, nor the ear hear from itself but from that, the sensual man does not apprehend."

3

CHAPTER IX.

A VIEW OF THE WORKING FORCES OF THE UNIVERSE.

ASTRONOMY began with solid Crystalline Spheres; then the theory of Epicycles was adopted; after which Descartes introduced the Vortices; then the discovery of Gravitation arrived through Newton; and now, within all and above all, the world is enriched with Polarization, by which chemical, electrical, magnetic, and even mechanical forces, are wedded by beautiful reciprocations and most intimate relationships; and thus the whole subject of the working forces of the universe becomes more than ever attractive and fruitful.

There are two most important discoveries in science: First, the universal persistency and indestructibility of Force; and second, the interpolarity and universal convertibility of Force. The first, in modern scientific phraseology, is termed " the conservation of force," and the last " the correlation of force "—teaching the divine lesson that all forces, as well as all forms in the Universe, are immortal sisters and brothers.

From these splendid discoveries, the illustrations of which need not be given here, we obtain the stellar key to the Summer Land. Force is as substantial, as real, as material, as matter itself; nay, more, the materialism of matter melts away and utterly disappears in the spiritualism of intelligent principles! Dr. Joule, of England, has demonstrated the mechanical equivalence of *heat*, which, hitherto in science, has been considered material, but is now seen to be only another form of force. Nature's Divine Revelations, published long before these discoveries, teach the *materiality* of " Fire," " Heat," " Light," " Electricity," " Magnetism," " Motion," " Life," " Sensation," " Intelligence," and, highest of all, " Spirit." And for teaching *such* "materialism," the whole religious and literary world was provoked to opposition and ridicule. But, according to progressive law, Prof. Faraday demonstrates the material immateriality, so to speak, of electricity, and shows the intimate relationships and equivalence of electrical and chemical forces; and very soon after it was found by Dr. Joule that " a pound weight falling through 772 feet, or 772 pounds falling through 1 foot, and then arrested, produce sufficient *heat* to raise one pound of water 1 degree of Fahrenheit." Thus a mechanical force is demonstrated as coming from what has been regarded as pure immateriality. And chemical and magnetic experiments, equally unquestionable, have established the spirituo-materiality of those elements which have been so long termed " imponderables." The next step must be into the realm whence forces emanate; into the very sacred presence of Intelligence, Will, Thoughts, Ideas, SPIRIT! And these, too, will have their equivalence and conversion into electrical force, into chemical force, into magnetic force, and into mechanical or lowest force; for SPIRIT IS SUBSTANCE; and every thing is rooted and grounded in Spirit; and so those extreme idealists, who have sentimentally and dogmatically abolished from the Summer Land all materiality, will be convinced that " something " could not have proceeded from " nothing ;" which discovery, doubtless, will greatly relieve them from many painful thoughts of possible annihilation.

Viewing the outlying and interior universes, with these new discoveries for spectacles, do you not apprehend a new scale of conservative and correlative forces? How does the following scale look? Begin at the bottom, with No. 1, and rise progressively, as a tree grows from its roots upward ; and then, having reached the topmost point of observation, let us pause and meditate :

9. DEITY.

8. IDEAS.

7. PRINCIPLES.

6. LAWS.

5. ESSENCES.

4. ETHERS.

3. VAPORS.

2. FLUIDS.

1. SOLIDS.

The lowest point of departure, No. 1, which is the plane of the " Solids," is the point where the highest substances and slowest motions are most demonstrated ; whilst the highest point attainable, No. 7, is where the lowest substance is most exalted, and in the highest possible state of motion and energy. No. 7 is the *positive* pole, and No. 1 the *negative* pole, of a perfect universe.

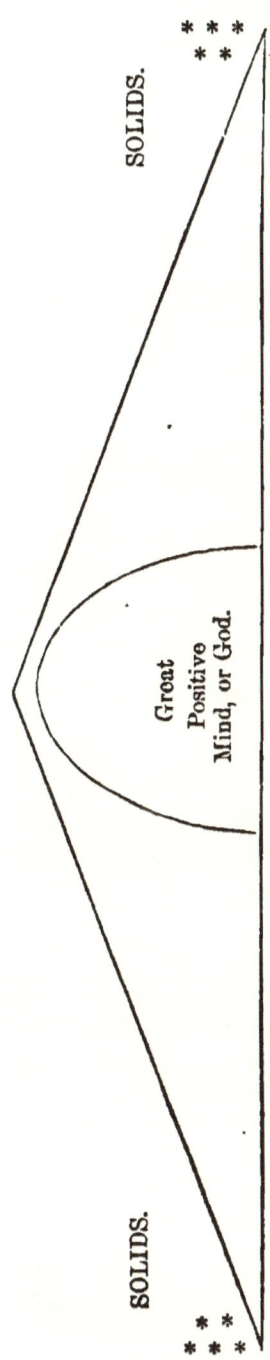

The philosophy of science, as modernly stated, is, practically, that "matter, viewed separately from force, is nothing." In other words, heat, light, electricity, magnetism, chemical effects, &c., are only different modes of motion or action of the same force. Different motions are said to be nothing but different expressions of force; transferred, in degrees of greater or less intensity, from one point to another point in space. It is by one popular scientific authority urged that "electricity, magnetism, and chemical affinity are correlates, and change readily into each other without loss of quantity of the original Force. These forces," he says, "or rather this force, since all are convertible, is the source of the delusion we are under with respect to matter, when we say we see and feel it. For what do we see? Light, which is force, photographs a minute inverted image on the bottom of the eye—on the retina, which acting on the brain produces consciousness of an object. All that is known to us is the mental conception—the *reality* of which our conception is composed, is Force.

It is evident there is no matter here. But surely we feel matter if we do not see it! The sense of Feeling is mere repulsion—resistance to motion. When we speak of matter as subtle, or as solid, liquid, or aëriform, we simply mean that it presents more or less resistance to motion. 'When the question arises,' says J. S. Mill, 'whether something which affects our senses in a peculiar way, as for instance whether Heat or Light, or Electricity, is or is not matter, what seems always to be meant is, does it offer any, however trifling, resistance to motion? If it were shown that it did, this would at once terminate all doubt.'

"But when we speak of either matter or force we speak only of the external cause of our sensations and ideas, and these tell us nothing of the real nature or essence of either; why not then continue to use the term matter, as heretofore? We answer, because the more general term force may include, and does really include, both what has hitherto been called Matter and Spirit also. We are told that 'Force viewed separately from matter is nothing.' I think it more correct to say that matter viewed separately from force is nothing, because we know that force passes into or changes into mind, as heat into light, and we thus include both sides of creation—Matter and Spirit. Force, in its different modes of action as Light, Heat, Electricity, Galvanism, Chemical Affinity, Attraction and Repulsion, is sufficient to produce half the phenomena around us. Life and Mind, which are correlates of Force, or other modes of its action, are sufficient to produce the other half. There is but One simple, primordial, absolute Force, with varying relations and conditions. The modes of ·

Force or Effects now in existence are neither more nor less than such as have previously existed, changed only in form. They have not merely acted upon each other, according to the common supposition with respect to matter, BUT HAVE CHANGED INTO EACH OTHER. This will be found to be a very important distinction. Each change is a new creation of something which in that form or mode has never existed before—a new life, and as it passes into another form or mode, a new death—'nothing repeats itself, because nothing can be placed again in the same condition : the past is irrevocable.' And may we not add, irrecoverable."

But while these philosophers are on the broad road that leadeth to a *forcible* annihilation of " Solids," they will discover, all of a sudden, in the straight and narrow way, that the *universe is essentially dual ;* and that the manifestations of force are only different forms or modes of a persistent and indestructible materiality, or the varying changes of an eternal substance, which is *negatively*, MATTER, and, *positively*, MIND—the two forms or conditions of the one unitary central Reality. The universal doubleness or duality of things is a demonstration of what is immutably true of the Central Whole.

The conservation and correlation of Forces, as the results in philosophic science are now denominated, require the admission that No. 7 and No. 1 in the scale, together with all the numbers between, are nothing but different forms or modes of a principle called " Force." Whereas, in accordance with our light on this subject, No. 7 comprehends and includes No. 1, as well as all the ascending numbers; but it is not possible that either should become the other, except in degree, and through the unceasing processes of spiral progression.

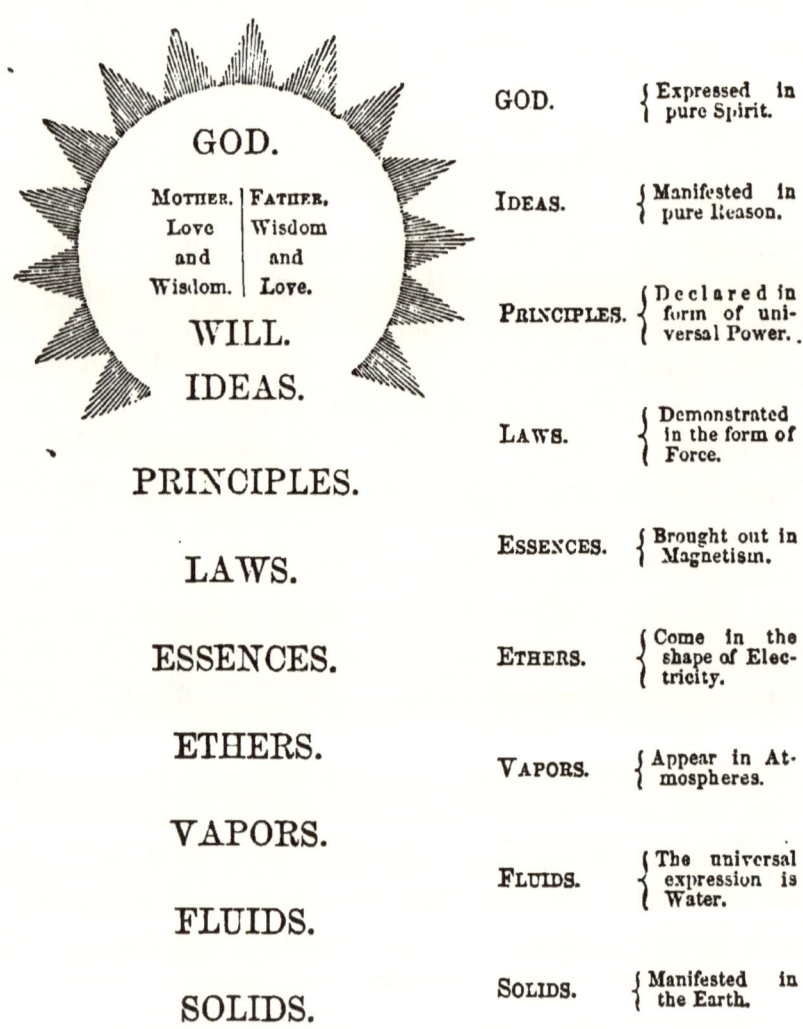

GOD.	Expressed in pure Spirit.
IDEAS.	Manifested in pure Reason.
PRINCIPLES.	Declared in form of universal Power.
LAWS.	Demonstrated in the form of Force.
ESSENCES.	Brought out in Magnetism.
ETHERS.	Come in the shape of Electricity.
VAPORS.	Appear in Atmospheres.
FLUIDS.	The universal expression is Water.
SOLIDS.	Manifested in the Earth.

Perhaps it would appear plainer if the scale were expressed as follows:—

CAUSES.	*Positive.*	SPIRIT—God;	The most perfect conception contains both Mother and Father.
		REASON—Ideas;	Both Love and Wisdom, contains all impersonal principles of God.
		POWER—Principles;	The unchangeable expressions of God's universal Ideas.
EFFECTS.	*Passive.*	FORCE—Laws;	The special methods of action of Ideas and Principles.
		MAGNETISM—Essences;	The vitalic utterances of Ideas, Principles, and Laws.
		ELECTRICITY—Ethers;	The universal medium for the manifestation of Ideas, Principles, Laws, and Essences.
ULTIMATES.	*Negative.*	ATMOSPHERE—Vapors;	The purifying laboratory through which flow the effects of Ideas, Principles, Laws, Essences, and Ethers.
		WATER—Fluids;	The viaduct for the transmission of the slowing motions of every substance and force in the universe.
		EARTH—Solids;	The lowest condition of Substance and the slowest utterance of Ideas, Principles, Laws, Essences, Ethers, Vapors, and Fluids.

It may not be deemed inappropriate to present still another scale and statement. The subject may possibly be brought yet closer to the common understanding.

3*

We will give the genesis of the world-building descension of the Divine Substance, thus:—

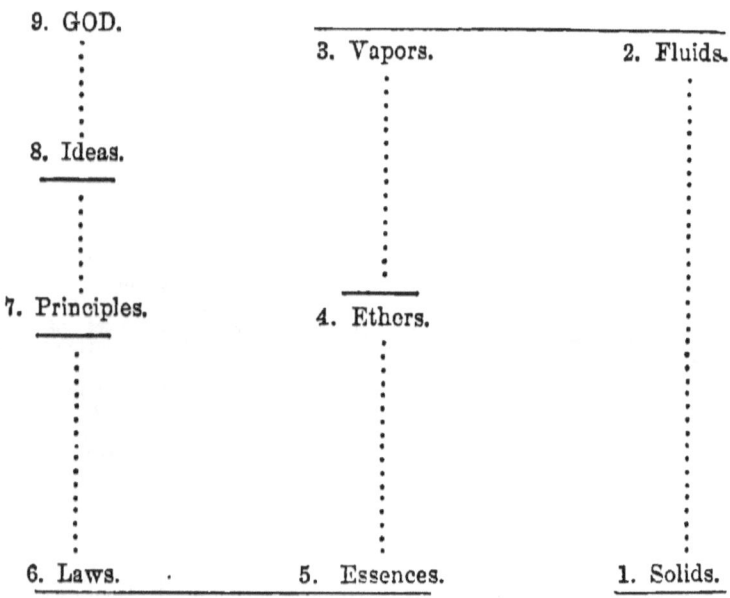

The plane of Solids is reached by the continuous degrees of descending action of the primordial positive Powers. Although these degrees appear dissimilar and discreted, or separated by impassable barriers of wholly dissimilar parts of the causative Energy; yet the acknowledged sovereign law of convertibility or correlation of forces and substances, must convince the rational intelligence that "discrete degrees," in the absolute sense, are impossible in a universe constructed upon an infinite number of inseparable affinities.

In the amazing magnitude of our subject, so opulent of variety and so fruitful in thought, the mind is constantly liable to lose the links of the argument. The vagueness of the hints about resolving all matter into force, is, of itself, sufficient to perplex and fatigue the non-scientific understanding. But calmness of brain will keep the thinking faculties in receptive condition.

Of God, Spinoza says: "He is the Universal Being, of which all things are the manifestations." Hegel also defines God as the " Being," or, perhaps, in philosophic language, as the "Central Causation." Huxley says that " every form is force become visible; a form of rest is a balance of forces; a form undergoing change is the predominance of one over others." In a more reverential temper Prof. Tyndall says: " We know no more of the origin of force than of the origin of matter; where matter is, force is, for we only know matter through its forces." In his very scholarly work on Heat, he grandly put the whole question thus:—

" The discoveries and generalizations of modern science constitute a poem more sublime than has ever yet been addressed to the imagination. The natural philosopher of to-day may dwell amid conceptions which beggar those of Milton. So great and grand are they, that in the contemplation of them a certain force of character is requisite to preserve us from bewilderment. Look at the integrated energies of our world—the stored power of our coal-fields, or winds and rivers, our fleets, armies, and guns. What are they? They are all generated by a portion of the sun's energy, which does not amount to one thousand three hundred millionth part of the whole. This is the entire fraction of the sun's force intercepted by the Earth, and we convert but a small fraction of this fraction into mechanical energy. Multiplying all our powers by millions of millions, we do not reach the sun's expenditure. And still, notwith-

standing this enormous drain, in the lapse of human
history we are unable to detect a diminution of his store.
Measured by our largest terrestrial standards, such a
reservoir of power is infinite; but it is our privilege to
rise above these standards, and to regard the sun himself as a speck in infinite extension, a mere drop in the
universal sea. We analyze the space in which he is
immersed, and which is the vehicle of his power. We
pass to other systems and other suns, each pouring forth
energy like our own, but still without infringements of
the law, which reveals immutability in the midst of
change, which recognizes incessant transference, conversion, but neither final gain nor loss. This law general-
izes the aphorism of Solomon, that there is nothing new
under the sun, by teaching us to detect everywhere,
under its infinite variety of appearances, *the same primeval force.* To nature nothing can be added; from
nature nothing can be taken away; the sum of her
energies is constant, and the utmost man can do in
the pursuit of physical truth, or in the application of
physical knowledge, is to shift the constituents of the
never-varying total. The law of conservation rigidly
excludes both creation and annihilation. Waves may
change to ripples, and ripples to waves—magnitude may
be substituted for number, and number for magnitude—
asteroids may aggregate to suns, suns may resolve themselves into floræ and faunæ and floræ and faunæ melt
into air—the flux of power is eternally the same, it rolls
in music through the ages, and all terrestrial energy—
the manifestations of life as well as the display of phenomena—are but modulations."

The application and weight of all this scientific testimony will be seen and felt when we come to "sum up the evidence." A few more points must be first made clear to reason. According to our scale the materialist might say: "Mind, in its slowest and lowest condition, is matter; and the reverse, matter, in its loftiest form of motion and highest condition, is mind." But this is not our meaning; nor is it true, in any logical sense. Our philosophy is, that the universe is a two-fold unity —two eternal manifestations of two substances, which, at heart, are One, but eternally *twain* in the realms of Cause and Effect. In the absence of better words, these two Substances we term Matter and Mind—interchangeable, convertible, essentially identical, eternally harmonious, wedded by the polarities of positive and negative forces.

Recalling our scale of nine steps in the ascending and descending processes of Mind and Matter, you will perceive that "Essence" is the connecting "link" between the Positive and the Negative hemispheres, thus :—

POSITIVE.	PASSIVE.	NEGATIVE.
1. 2. 3. 4.	5.	6. 7. 8. 9.

GOD, IDEAS, PRINCIPLES, LAWS, ESSENCES, ETHERS, VAPORS, FLUIDS, SOLIDS.

The region of "Essences" is the region of "magnetisms." This, then, is the true "link" in the chain, which unites the positive side or "mind" to the "negative" side or "matter;" but, in a finer analysis, it will be found more correct to term matter and mind "Spirit," with two forms of manifestation ; thus relieving " matter " of the epithet of " grossness," and reclaiming " mind " from its long exilement in the awful solitudes of unapproachable immateriality.

Let us recapitulate, and thus ascertain the information obtained :

1. The *rotundity* of all bodies in space ;

2. The *circularity* of the motions of all bodies ;

3. The existence of *zones* in the planetary organization ;

4. The *harmony* of relationship between the exterior and interior universes ;

5. The *polarity* of all forms and forces in nature ;

6. The *descent* of Spirit to Earth, and the *ascent* of Earth to Spirit.

7. The *eternity* and the *unity* of both hemispheres of the univercœlum.

Now, in order to ascertain the possibility, the probability, and the *certainty* of the Summer Land Zone, we must logically follow Nature's pathway from the region of causes to the region of effects. Her unalterable code is plainly and universally indicated, namely, — *forms visible are effects which flow from corresponding causes invisible.* A man's body, for example, is the effect of an *interior* organizing, vivifying, sustaining, spiritual individuality. It elaborated his brain, his heart, his organs, his senses, and indeed all parts of his physical temple ; although each part may have been modified, and generally is modified and twisted more or less by parental instrumentalities and circumstantial influences both before and after birth.

Now apply this principle to the organization of the vast Stellar Universe. What gave to matter the universal tendency to form globes?—to roll out into immense zones?—to stratify and continue for innumerable ages as revolving belts?—to move in circular paths through the solitudes of immensity? There is but one answer: The spiritual universe is composed of globes, of zones, and of belts, which move harmoniously in wavy circles of causation through the vaster, deeper, higher, more interior heavens of unimaginable infinitude. Men look through telescopes, and discern nothing but the outermost materialized garments of *hidden* corresponding spiritualized spheres of light, warmth, beauty, fertility, peace, progression, and happiness. There is just as much *certainty* that the Summer Land exists as that your mind exists; for it exists and your mind exists upon the one eternal law of cause and effect. Your body is a demonstration of an interior antecedent corresponding formative individuality; so the solar system exists, a demonstration of an interior antecedent corresponding formative spiritual universe.

CHAPTER X.

THE PRINCIPLES OF THE FORMATION OF THE SUMMER LAND.

THE order of the universe is as perfect as its varieties are innumerable. The principles engaged in forming worlds are incessantly engaged in decomposing them. In no other way can perpetual youth be bestowed upon the finer bodies and spheres of space. Atoms sufficiently refined to ascend above the mineral compound, enter into the forms of vegetable life. Vegetation, in its turn, delegates its finest atoms to enter and build up the animal kingdom. The most refined animal atoms enter into and support human bodies. And the most refined particles of human bodies, which are not required to construct and support the "garment of immortality," ascend to form the solids, fluids, and ethers of that effulgent Zone to which all human beings are incessantly hastening. Thus the eternal youthfulness, the healthful and beautiful juvenility, of the spiritual universe are established and immutably maintained. And now behold the philosophical, the geometrical, the musical, the harmonial grandeur and gloriousness of the beautiful WHOLE :—

GOD.

MOTHER. / FATHER.

LOVE & WISDOM—WILL—WISDOM & LOVE.

SPIRIT Pos. { ☞

MATTER Neg. { The Fountain! Here atoms receive the omnipotent centrifugal impulsion to go forth.

SPIRIT Pos. { ☞   The Highest Summer Land in the Spiritual Universe.

MATTER Neg. { In this belt all matter is a boundless rotating ocean of Fire, Heat, Light, Electricity, and Magnetism, containing all Forces.

SPIRIT Pos. { ☞   A Celestial Inhabited Sphere " Nearer, my God, to Thee."

MATTER Neg. { The unimaginable ocean of chemical substance has cut new channels in space; yet all revolving like cohesive seas of Fire and Force.

SPIRIT Pos. { ☞   A More Interior Summer Land.

MATTER Neg. { In this belt of cosmical matter the vast masses of solar atoms are sufficiently cool to separate, to obey the law of cohesion, and to organize suns.

SPIRIT Pos. { ☞   A Higher Summer Land.

MATTER Neg. { This is a broad zone of inter-cohesive cometary and meteoric nuclei, containing no stratified orbs. It is perfectly illustrated by the present condition of Saturn's rings.

SPIRIT Pos. { ☞   The Summer Land, which all enter at death.

MATTER Neg. { This represents the gorgeous Galaxy visible in the heavens spanning from northeast to southwest, called "The Milky Way." Some of its suns are distant more than 19,250,000,000,000 miles. Our sun and planets belong to this belt.

*Sun
Earth

The Spiritual Spheres have been recently termed Summer Lands, and there are, counting man's earthly existence the *first* sphere of spirit life, in all *six* spheres in the ascending flight toward Deity, who fills the Seventh Sphere, and is infinitely greater than millions of such univercœlums as man can conceive.

Observe this universal and unerring *law* of the Supernal Administration : The Central Positive Power *repels the physical*, and at the same moment *attracts the spiritual ;* therefore the circulation of matter is from the center outward, whilst spirit travels from the outside toward the center. These two reciprocal processes, or opposite currents, are incessantly flowing. The inconceivable oceans of world-building materials expand and swell, and pour outwardly from the eternally flowing and inexhaustible Fountain at the center ; at the same time the innumerable multitudes of individualized spiritual and angelic men, women, and children, from off all the human-bearing planets in space, are progressively and irresistibly marching inwardly toward the great positive attractive Center, and constantly approaching nearer and nearer the eternal sun-sphere of Father and Mother !

The formation of the different Summer Lands can be seen in the principles which unrolled like an infinite scroll the suns and stars of the serene firmament. Whence comes the power, asks Prof. Tyndall, on the part of the molecules, to compel the solar energy to take determinate forms ? Water may be raised from the sea-level to a high elevation, and then permitted to descend. In descending it may be made to assume various forms—to fall in cascades, to spirt in fountains, to boil in eddies, or to flow tranquilly along a uniform bed. It may, moreover, be caused to set complex machinery in motion, to turn millstones, throw shuttles, work saws and hammers, and drive piles. But every form of power here indicated would be derived from the original power expended in raising the water to the height from which it fell. There is no energy *generated* by the machinery; the work performed by the water in descending is merely the parceling out and distribution of the work expended in raising it. In precisely this sense is all the energy of plants and animals the parceling out and distribution of a power originally exerted by the sun. In the case of the water, the source of the power consists in the forcible separation of a quantity of the liquid from the lowest level of the earth's surface, and its elevation to a higher position, the power thus expended being returned by the water in its descent.

In the case of vital phenomena, the source of power consists in the forcible separation of the atoms of chemical compounds by the sun—of the carbon and hydrogen, for example, of the carbonic acid and water diffused throughout the atmosphere, from the oxygen with which they are combined. This separation is effected in the leaves of plants by solar energy. The constituents of the carbonic acid and water are there torn asunder in spite of their mutual attraction, the carbon and hydrogen are stored up in the wood, and the oxygen is set free in the air. When the wood is burned the oxygen recombines with the carbon, and the heat then given out is of the precise amount drawn from the sun to effect the previous "reduction" of the carbonic acid. The reunion of the carbon with the oxygen is similar to the reunion of our falling water with the earth from which it had been separated. We name the one action "gravity" and the other "chemical affinity;" but these different names must not mislead us regarding the qualitative identity of the two forces. They are both *attraction*, and, to the intellect, the falling of carbon atoms against oxygen atoms is not more difficult of conception than the falling of water to the earth.

It is generally supposed that our earth once belonged to the sun, from which it was detached in a molten condition. Hence arises the question, " Did that incandescent world contain latent within itself the elements of life ?" Or, supposing a planet carved from our present sun, and set spinning around him at the distance of our earth, would one of the consequences of its refrigeration be the development of organic forms ? *Structural* forces certainly lie latent in the molten mass, whether or not those forces reach to the extent of forming a plant or an animal. All the marvels of crystalline force, all those wonderful branching frost-ferns which cover our window-panes on a winter morning—the exquisite molecular architecture which is now known to belong to the ice of our frozen lakes—all this 'constructiveness' lies latent in an amorphous drop of water, and comes into play when the water is sufficiently cooled. And who will set limits to the possible play of molecular forces in the cooling of a planet ?

Thus the teaching of science is, that the world-constructing forces are "latent in the mass," and that the formation of a dew-drop is not less wonderful than the formation of an inhabitable world.   The formation of spiritualized material belts is a proceeding in the universe as natural and rational as the formation of the primordial rings out of which all the planets, satellites, and lesser bodies were subsequently developed.

But will not the Spiritual Zones be broken up and distributed through space by counter attractions?   The spiritual belts cannot be drawn asunder by an exterior and superior attraction; for they are, as we shall hereafter show, constituted of ultimate or final particles, which entertain only very remote affinities for the particles and constituents of other bodies in space.

But the question may arise, " Why is not the Summer Land *round*, like a globe, rather than in the shape of a vast Zone or stratified belt?"

Geometry gives the true answer to this question. This exact and deathless science brings to light the *figures*, or the forms and shapes, possible to and revealed by material bodies.   By geometrical principles, all the varieties and possibilities of figures in crystalline and other bodies can be fully comprehended and determined.

The fundamental law of Nature, in every department of her organization, seems to be this: The beginning and the ending—the Alpha and the Omega—are in perfect and complete correspondence.   The two extremes meet, facing one another, and thus they embrace; each seeing his own perfect image and perfect likeness in the other!   The representation and correspondence—the exactness of similitude in outline and in all the details —are marvelous in their mathematical and geometrical

perfections. Thus, in very truth, "extremes meet"—
primate and ultimate—acorn buried in the ground re-
appearing in acorn on the topmost bough of the oak—a
truth exemplified in every growth-circle of vegetable,
animal, and human life; and in the repetitions of
national history no less than in the incessant recurrence
of public crises, and in the periodicities of individual
experience.

Apply this law to the primordial structure of the stellar
universe. What was the *first* figure, what the *primary*
form, in which matter appeared? Was it originally
globular? That is, Were the first world-building forms
round, like immense balls, or were they spheroidal
belts of cosmical matter? Let us take testimony of
Prof. Kirkwood. He adopts the nebular hypothesis
as the most rational explanation of things, and so declares that the "sun was an exceedingly diffused, rotating nebula, of spherical or *spheroidal* form, extending
beyond the orbit of the most distant planet; the planets
as yet having no separate existence. This immense
sphere of vapor, in consequence of the radiation of heat
and the continual action of gravity, became gradually
more dense, which condensation was necessarily attended
by an increased angular velocity of rotation. At length
a point was thus reached where the centrifugal force of
the equatorial parts was equal to the central attraction.
The condensation of the interior meanwhile continuing,
the equatorial zone was detached, but necessarily continued to revolve around the central mass with the
same velocity that it had at the epoch of its separation.
*If perfectly uniform throughout its entire circum-
ference, it would continue its motion in an unbroken*

ring, like that of Saturn; if not, it would probably collect into several masses, having orbits nearly identical. These masses should assume a spheroidal form, with a rotary motion in the direction of that of their revolution, because their inferior particles have a less real velocity than the superior; they have therefore constituted so many planets in a state of vapor. But if one of them was sufficiently powerful to unite successively by its attraction all the others about its center, the ring of vapors would be changed into one *spheroidal* mass, circulating about the sun, with a motion of rotation in the same direction with that of revolution."

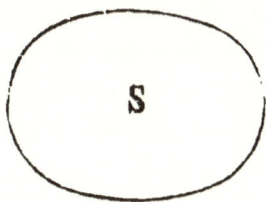

THE PRIMAL FORM.

The testimony of popular astronomical science therefore is : *The primary figure was spheroidal.* The oval form, consequently, is the beginning form of matter—its genesis and its exodus also. The original oval or ellipsis is not elongated, remember, is not drawn out, but, instead, is *shortened,* so as to produce an almost geometrically perfect circle, yet always *inclined* to the elliptic. The globe-form, which is the perfectly round or sphere-form, is not possible in a body which constantly and rapidly revolves in one direction. The earth, consequently, is bulged at the equator and correspondingly flattened at the poles. So of all the planets, satellites, and minor bodies of space. The law of infallible geometry is: *The climactric form of matter is spheroidal.* The broad belt of the Summer Land is the highest form of spiritualized atoms—the ultimate and divinest figure—the final shape of all perfectly attenuated and exalted cosmical matter.

Take, for a further illustration, the scale of sounds in the exact science of music. Between the first or lowest note and the eighth or highest note, we find all the possible intermediate sounds. But the eighth note and the first note are essentially the *same;* or, in other words, the last sound is a perfect reiteration or repro-duction of the first sound; and it is also the *basis* of an-other and a higher, but exactly similar scale, adapted to the measurement of higher sounds; and so onward and upward, progressively, like the steps in a flight of stairs, until you attain to as high a sound as can be developed by the human voice. This harmonial law of progres-sive reproduction—the first becoming last, and the last first—will answer the question concerning the zone-shape of the Summer Land.

Unsearchable and incomprehensible as this law of correspondence may appear at first sight, yet nothing can be more easily read when your senses, intelligence, and wisdom unite for work, and seriously devote them-selves to the examination. By no other law can man perfectly acquire knowledge of those harmonial ties by which all and each of the pieces and parts of the uni-verse are fastened together. Poets, in moments of intuitive exaltation, *feel* more than the common intelli-gei ce can grasp :—

> " Are not the mountains, waves, and skies a part
> Of me and of my soul, as I of them?

Is not the love of these deep in my heart
With a pure passion ?"

In music, which we have taken for an illustration, how exactly mathematical in all its parts, from which flow innumerable spiritualizing qualities, effects, and enchantments. All art-music is suggested by, derived from, and unerringly governed by nature—the source of all melody and harmony. The term " discord " in music does not mean confusion and antagonism. Discord, accord, and modulation form the august trinity. The accord of contrasted sounds—the mathematical combination and the unitary development of individual discordant notes—unfolds perfect harmony !

External music reaches the spirit-ear through the wave-undulations of the invisible ether of space. A sound is increased in proportion to the number of vibrations per second ; thus, " the lowest note of a 7-octave piano is made by 32 vibrations per second, the highest by 7.680, while each intermediate note has its fixed number." The pitch of a note is ascertained, and the number of its vibrations per second determined by its position on the five parallel lines termed " the staff." And it is another beautiful miracle (surprise ?) in music, that the *deepest* natural note, which can only be reached by man's voice, is E, below the line of the second staff, and the *highest* natural note, which can only be sounded by a woman's voice, is designated E, above the first staff. There is in this beautiful adaptation a progression of voices just *three masculines and three feminines;* man represents and develops the " base," the " baritone,"² and the " tenor," whilst woman unfolds the three higher refinements, a greater number of sound

4

waves per second, in the "contralto" and "soprano," the highest notes of which only woman's voice can reach. Byron speaks of—

> "The soul and source of music, which makes known
>   Eternal harmony, and sheds a charm
> Like to the fabled Cytherea's zone,
>   Blending all things with beauty; 'twould disarm
> The spectre Death, had he substantial power to harm."

It is a wonderful demonstration of the inherent genius of man's mind, that in a concert of music a good ear can attend to the different parts of the music *separately*, or *to all at once !* "In the latter case," says the metaphysician, Sir William Hamilton, "the mind is constantly varying its attention from one part to the other; the rapidity of its operations giving no perceptible interval of time." What are the facts in this example? In a musical concert we have a multitude of different instruments and voices, emitting at once an infinity of different sounds. These all reach the ear at the same indivisible moment in which they perish, and, consequently, if heard at all—much more if their mutual relation or harmony be perceived—they must be all heard simultaneously. This is evident. For if the mind can attend to each minimum of sound only successively, it consequently requires a minimum of time in which it is exclusively occupied with each minimum of sound. Now in this minimum of time there coexist with it, and with it perish, many minima of sound which, *ex hypothesi*, are not perceived, are not heard, as not attended to. In a concert, therefore, on this doctrine, a small number of sounds only could be perceived, and above this petty maximum all sounds would be to the ear as zero. But what is the fact? No concert, however numerous its instruments, has yet been found to have reached, far less to have surpassed, the capacity of the mind and its organ. How perfectly true it is that—

> 'Nature sounds the music of the spirit;
> Sweetly to her worshiper she sings,
> All the glow, the grace she doth inherit,
> Round her trusting child she fondly flings."

According to the reproductive law, a broad, effulgent, rotating belt or zone is the *first figure* or form revealed in the geometrical music scale of world-building in the Stellar Universe; so also is it the highest and *last figure* or form of which matter, in its most exalted condition of ethereal and essential refinement, is capable of assuming; and thus, consequently and logically, we actually find organized and revolving all the ascending succession of Spheres in the constitution of the univercœlum!

And what is most remarkable and memorable is, that the seven ascending scales of Spiritual Zones, with their intervals of suns and planets, were discerned and described by the author, just as they were seen before he lived, and as they have been frequently perceived and pictured by others since his first account was published. And each seer was separate from and independent of the other not only, but the positive existence and identical structure of the Spheres were discovered and described by each without any external knowledge or hint of the sublime geometrical law; which law, you now perceive, is at once an infallible explanation and an incontrovertible demonstration, that the physical universe is *spheroidal* in shape, that it is composed of a progressive series of successively ascending *circles* of suns and planets, and that it is nothing but the covering, the material garment, the organized *body* of that more interior and spiritual universe which was "not made with hands, eternal in the heavens."

CHAPTER XI.

DEMONSTRATIONS OF THE HARMONIES OF THE UNIVERSE.

THE Harmonial Philosophy of the universe would receive vast aid from the demonstrations of mathematical and geometrical science, but this is not the place to introduce such elaborate calculations and convincing measurements as are impatient to take the stand as positive witnesses. We hope that minds gifted with mathematical and geometrical knowledge will feel moved to enter upon this enchanting inquiry. Science gives definite conceptions of the order and wisdom of the universe. Pythagoras, Plato, Euclid, Apollonius, Archimedes, Ptolemy, Kepler, Newton— all great men in the science of Geometry, and therefore all were great believers in the order and unchangeable goodness of the infinite system.

Most minds, however, find satisfaction in analogical reasoning, in contrasts, in correspondential and symbolical forms of thought, and in this manner perceive the glory and application of great principles. For such, more intuitive idealists, who do not like the rigid exactness of geometrical "fluxions," "conic sections," "differential calculus," &c., I am impressed to adopt and present a variety of scales which are not less truthful than mathematics, while they are far more effective with the great mass of minds.

NEGATIVE. POSITIVE.

IDEAS.

NEGATIVE. POSITIVE.

PRINCIPLES.

NEGATIVE. POSITIVE.

LAWS.

NEGATIVE. POSITIVE.

ESSENCES.

NEGATIVE. POSITIVE.

ETHERS, VAPORS, FLUIDS, SOLIDS.

NEGATIVE. POSITIVE.

The four primal forms of motion and matter are expressed at the foundation in Ethers, Vapors, Fluids, Solids. The modern discovery of science, that *polarity* is inseparable from the various conditions of matter, serves our purpose from every possible point of observation. The simplicity of the last scale will seem more profound from a more elaborate presentation. The two columns of "Positives" and "Negatives" may assist your mind to a still clearer conception of Nature's infinite interlacings of harmony.

The term "Earth," in our scales, is employed in the general sense, and not with reference merely to the planet on which we live. Earth is earth, as much on Juno as on Venus; earth is earth, as much on Vesta and the Moon as on Neptune, and the term is applicable to all the more remote bodies in our solar community.

The word, therefore, is used to signify that state of matter, anywhere in the universe, which is known as the coldest in temperature and the *lowest* in the degree of atomic motion. Truly has it been said, that the hollow ball on which we live contains within itself the elements of its own destruction. Within the outer crust—the cool temperature of which supports animal and vegetable life, and solidifies the stone, coal and metallic ores so important, to our well-being—there exists a mass of fluid igneous matter. Some of this matter occasionally escapes through the mouth of a volcano, or makes its presence felt by an earthquake; but neither the earthquake nor the volcano is necessary to prove that fire exists in the earth. At the depth of 2,480 yards, water boils; lead melts at the depth of 3,400 yards. There is red heat at the depth of seven

	EXPLANATION.	POSITIVE.	NEGATIVE.
The Sphere of MIND.	The fountain Source of all Laws, Forces, Principles, Ideas, is universally called ☞	GOD.	SPIRIT.
	The universality of motion, heat, light, life, sensation, order, beauty, intelligence, love, will, wisdom, reveal ☞	IDEAS.	REASON.
	The uniformity and universality of these laws of cause and effect unfold the higher revelations of mind, called ☞	PRINCIPLES.	POWER.
	The first manifestation of Mind is Motion; the effect of Force; and the modes of the actions of this Motion are termed ☞	LAWS.	FORCE.
The essence of magnetism is the link connecting mind with matter.	Ether-atoms are atoms in the highest possible degree of motion, constituting an infinitely rare medium, chemical, dynamic, elastic, and all-pervading, called ☞	ESSENCES.	MAGNETISM.
The Sphere of MATTER.	The vapor-atoms ascend one degree higher in the scale and expand throughout all space with an increase of motion, and are termed ☞	ETHERS.	ELECTRICITY.
	The fluid-atoms receive an increase motion with an increase of temperature, cohesion is overcome, and they expand into the condition known as ☞	VAPORS.	ATMOSPHERE.
	The solidity and cohesion of the same atoms disappear when they are visited by a given quantity of motion; heat is developed, and those become ☞	FLUIDS.	WATER.
	Atoms, when slowest in motion and coldest in temperature, drop into a compact body, for which the general term is ☞	SOLIDS.	EARTH.

miles, and if we adopt the temperature as calculated by Morveau's corrected scale of Wedgeworth's pyrometer, we find that the earth is fluid at the depth of one hundred miles.

Beautiful heavenly harmony is displayed in all the realms of being. Luminous fountains flow full of eternal ideas, rolling the universe in harmonious splendors. The templed perfections of God shine throughout the mountains of Truth.

Great souls are filled with love,
 Great brows are calm;
Serene within their might, they soar above
 The whirlwind and the storm.

In *words* the Godly man is mute—
 In *deeds* he lives—
Wouldst know the tree? examine well the fruit!
 The flower? the scent it gives!

Great thoughts are still as stars,
 Great thoughts are high;
They grasp the soul where 'neath the prison bars
 It languidly doth lie.

They bring it forth on wings
 Sublime and grand!
Where in the night of deeply-hidden things
 It joyfully doth expand.

Like sentinels they stand,
 And softly keep
Their silent watches, where a ruthless band
 Of lurking errors creep.

Like pearls of starry light
 That burn and glow,
They pierce the shadowy vail, and o'er the night
 Their mystic splendors throw.

4*

Great truths! ah, yes, more grand,
 More light and high,
Than hopes that thrill the wires throughout the land!
 Than stars that gem the sky!

Great truths! ah, yes, more fair,
 Sublime and deep,
Than burning thoughts that tremble on the air!
 Than the mysteries of sleep!

From nature's Soul they spring
 To joy and light,
And on imagination's quivering wing
 They take their onward flight.

In beauty's garb they rise,
 All fresh as morn,
And on their pinions, spread for sunlit skies,
 Our souls are gladly borne.

With myriad wrongs they wage
 An endless war;
And shed their luster o'er each passing age,
 Like Morning's golden star.

Great truths! they come from God!
 In heaven have birth;
They spring to life from each prophetic word
 That thrills the earth!

The correspondence between Mind and Matter, and
the beautiful progressions in the scale of colors, with
their many and diversified polarizations, is as perfect and
self-evident as any sum in mathematics. Commence
at the bottom of the scale, " Red," and ascend to the
climax in that color, " White," which is the garment of
omniscient Jehovah, and the emblem among human
angels of purity, fidelity, and truth. " Light," in this

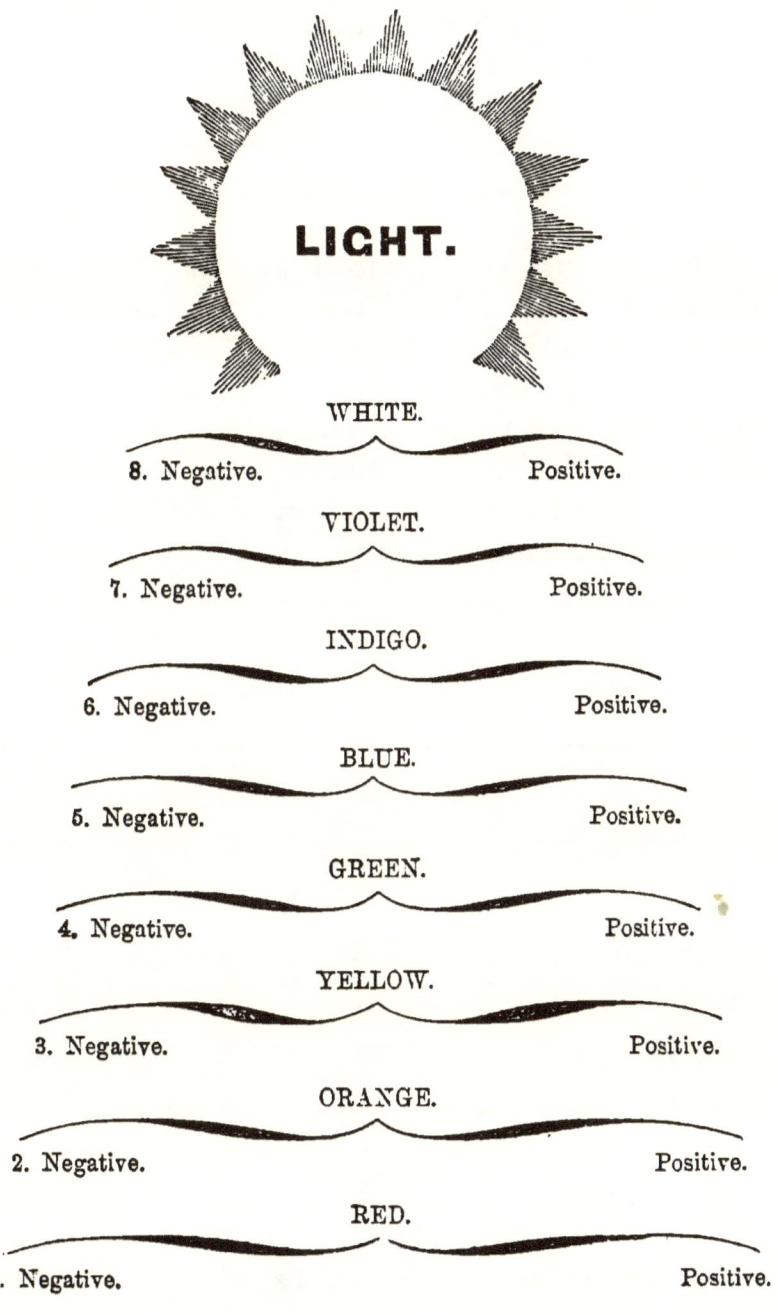

LIGHT.

WHITE.

8. Negative.   Positive.

VIOLET.

7. Negative.   Positive.

INDIGO.

6. Negative.   Positive.

BLUE.

5. Negative.   Positive.

GREEN.

4. Negative.   Positive.

YELLOW.

3. Negative.   Positive.

ORANGE.

2. Negative.   Positive.

RED.

1. Negative.   Positive.

musical scale of colors, occupies the throne of God in the other scale, and in each you find the 3–6–9 points in geometrical ratio, or the 3 times 3, by which the whole system is demonstrated to be correlated parts of one harmonious manifestation of infinite wisdom and love.

Who can with *indifference* behold all this sublime harmony? The child of Nature is overwhelmed with wonder and happiness. The spirit of God enters your understanding, ascends the throne of your reason, and declares the whole gospel of philosophical truth. Look at the scale of colors from another point of observation, by which we learn of the wondrous activities of the principles of Light.

SCALE OF THE SEVEN COLORS.	*Wave lengths in* 10 *millionths of an inch.*	*Number of undulations per inch.*	*Number of undulations per second in Billions.*
1. RED..................	266	37.640	458
2. ORANGE	240	41.610	506
3. YELLOW	227	44.000	535
4. GREEN	211	47.460	577
5. BLUE	196	51.110	622
6. INDIGO	185	54.070	658
7. VIOLET	167	59.750	727

In the previous scale it was found that "Essences," which are eliminated and revealed in the forms of force called "magnetism," is the *middle* principle—the link connecting the sphere of Mind with the sphere of Matter.

Positive.			Passive.	Negative.		
White.	Violet.	Indigo.	Green.	Yellow.	Orange.	Red.
(7.)	(6.)	(5.)	(4.)	(3.)	(2.)	(1.)

The same law of correspondence appears in the natural classification and polarization of colors; showing that " Green " is the connecting link between the three majors and the three minors. Remember that, in all the scales we introduce, the *first* is the *lowest* and most inferior; and our true meaning is never seen unless the ascent is intellectually made from the bottom, up; or from the figure " 1," to the highest in the scale, just as you naturally walk up a flight of stairs, or as a tree grows upward from its germ-genesis in the soil below.

It is not generally known that Swedenborg anticipated Goethe's Theory of Colors.* In the *Arcana*, § 1042, he writes : " In order to the existence of color, there must needs be some substance darkish and brightish, or black and white, on which, when the rays of light from the sun fall, according to the various temperature of the dark and bright, or black and white, from the modification of the influent rays of light, there exist colors, some of which take more or less from the darkish and black, some more or less from the brightish and white, and hence arises their diversity."

---

* Persons have objected to, and treated as simple and childish, the introduction of colors in the form of badges and emblems, in the " Children's Progressive Lyceum," on the supposition that there is no interior educational significance in colors. Let such minds ask God *why* colors exist !

The positive "white," and the negative, "black," was apprehended by Swedenborg as the natural basis, in the intervals of which, as between the first and eighth note in music, all the varieties and tints of colors appear. In like manner, and upon the same principle of unerring correspondence, we affirm that in the interval between " Earth," *negative*, and " Spirit," *positive*, all the diversified wonders of Matter and Mind are unfolded.

An expositor of Swedenborg's philosophy of the phenomenal universe—which seem to exist without and to press up against our bodily senses—thus, as a kind of synopsis, states the grand idealism of his revered master :—

" What we call Nature, meaning by that term the universe of existence, mineral, vegetable, and animal, which seems to us infinite in point of space and eternal in point of time, is yet in itself, or absolutely, void both of infinity and eternity; the former appearance being only a sensible product and correspondence of a relation which the universal heart of man is under to the Divine Love, and the latter, a product and correspondence of the relation which the universe of the human mind is under to the Divine Wisdom. Thus Nature is not in the least what it sensibly purports to be, namely, absolute and independent; but, on the contrary, is at every moment, both in whole and in part, a pure phenomenon or effect of spiritual causes as deep, as contrasted, and yet as united, as God's infinite love and man's unfathomable want. In short, Swedenborg describes Nature as a perpetual outcome or product in the sphere of sense of an inward supersensuous marriage which is forever growing and forever adjusting itself between Creator and creature, between God's infinite and essential bounty and our infinite and essential necessity."

In this statement we regret that Swedenborg, or rather his intelligent pupil, employs the term "Nature" as synonymous with Earth or Matter. If this beautiful and indispensable word was used in the sense of that which expresses the eternal order and perfect beauty of the infinite Father and Mother, and in its place "Matter" be written, then we could most perfectly accept the philosophy as unquestionably true, because, in its essential points, it is exactly what we have been urging throughout these pages.

The positive and negative manifestations of color can be more clearly explained by a scale of what are called "complementary colors." These contrasts are the results of careful observation, analysis, and experimentation.

The sublime harmonies of the universe appear more and more as we extend our researches into the penetralium of causative principles. For example, man's five senses are organized progressively—each finer and higher than the other—corresponding with mathematical exactness to the five ascending degrees of matter.

Solid matter must be raised by expansion to the *fluid* condition before his tongue can *taste* it; solid matter must become *vapor* before his nose can *smell* it; solid matter must become *ether* before his ears can *hear* it; solid matter must become "essence" before his eyes can *see* it; but *solid* matter and man's *body* can meet, and *sensation* is elicited by resistance. The eyes do not see

the *ethereal* waves of sound; the ears do not perceive
the *magnetic* undulations of light; the olfactory nerves
do not realize the *fluid* condition of solids; neither does
the tongue taste the *vapors* (the atmosphere and odors)
which so readily record their presence upon the sense
of smell.

COMPLEMENTARY PARTS OR DIVISIONS OF LIGHT.

		POSITIVE.	NEGATIVE.
		WHITE.	BLACK.
Higher Series. {		Violet.	Yellow-Green.
		Indigo.	Orange-Yellow.
		Blue.	Orange-Red.
Intermediate or transitional. {		Green.	Reddish-Violet.
Lower Series. {		Yellow.	Indigo-Blue.
		Orange.	Azure-Blue.
		Red.	Bluish-Green.

The essences and ethers and vapors and fluids of
matter report themselves each to the appropriate sense.

In Matter as in Mind, we behold the unutterable harmonies of unerring Ideas, Principles, and Laws. The remarkable adjustments and adaptations of matter in its five conditions to man's five senses, must be obvious to every reflecting mind. Indeed, without such progressive ascensions and reciprocating polarizations of matter, man's reason and spirit could never arrive at any definite consciousness that there is a phenomenal world lying about him. The following scale of correspondences may bring these beautiful adaptations clearly into your understanding :—

FIVE SENSES.	FIVE FUNCTIONS.	FIVE CAUSES.	FIVE CONDITIONS.
5. Eyes ....Seeing	........Essences.......	Magnetism.	
4. Ears...........Hearing	.........Ethers.........	Electricity.	
3. Nose ....Smelling	.......Vapors.........	Atmosphere.	
2. Tongue ....Tasting	........Fluids.........	Water.	
1. Body ....Feeling	.........Solids.........	Earth.	

There is a yet more comprehensive generalization. See how beautifully harmonious ! Thus absolute Spirit is God ; in man, the miniature effect of the infinite cause comes out in Existence and Individuality. In the infinite, Ideas are the conscious principles of pure Reason ; in man, the finite effects ultimated and blossomed out, are Intuition and Intelligence. The fountain of causation, as it harmoniously flows outward and downward into human rivers of individualized life, may be tabulated thus :—

DIVINITY.				HUMANITY.	
FATHER.	MOTHER.			MAN.	WOMAN.
GOD	*is pure* SPIRIT	*ultimated in*		EXISTENCE *and*	INDIVIDUALITY.
IDEAS	*are divine* REASON	*manifested as*		INTELLECT *and*	INTUITION.
PRINCIPLES	*are pure* POWER	*known as motions*		CENTRIFUGAL *and*	CENTRIPETAL.
FORCES	*become* LAWS	*expressed as*		WILL *and*	PRODUCTION.

The principles of universal relationships reward richly all who study and comprehend them. Unless you *do* study them, you will not be convinced that the Spiritual Zone rests scientifically and philosophically upon the natural and indestructible order of the universe. You *must* study, or, at least, you ought to study, think, and reason, until you come to perceive and comprehend these grand progressive truths, namely: That the Solid world was once Fluid; that fluid was once Vapor; that vapor was once Ether; that ether was once Essence; that essence is the highest material connecting link for the operation of positive spiritual Laws; that these natural inherent laws constitute a negative medium for the manifestation of invisible celestial positive Force; that this force is the negative side of a yet more positive expression called Power; that this last potential demonstration is animated by interior intelligence and more positive energies termed Principles; that these immutable principles of the universe are external methods of positive, and still more interior, Ideas; that ideas are the self-thinking, inter-intelligent, purely-spiritual attributes and properties of the Divine Positive Mind.

And you should study and contemplate these grand truths until you perceive, as by the awakening and opening of your interior senses, that, from the innumerable multitude of stars down " to the lulled lake and mountain coast," all is concentered in a life of interlaced affinities and reciprocated relationships, " where not a beam, nor air, nor leaf is lost, but hath a part of being." Yes, you should think upon these inexhaustible glories until *deep thoughts* make you " silent," until you grow " breathless " with the immensity of high and holy feeling; yea, until in your open soul " all heaven and earth are still," while the life of your spirit blends its everlasting destiny with the eternally rolling splendors and indestructible unities of Truth.

But you must not "dream." For cold, exact Science, like the moon of truth—of which Philosophy is both sun and stars—walks over the earth and across the skies, heartlessly ; but he is armed with clean-cutting instruments of analysis and observation ; and so it will not avail you to turn away from Science because its ways are fatiguing, and idly bask your reason in the more congenial sunshine of generalization, below the silent spheres.

" Under the influence of passion," says Prof. Hamilton, the metaphysician, "men seek honor, but not truth. They do not cultivate what is most valuable in reality, but what is most valuable in opinion. They disdain, perhaps, what can be easily accomplished, and apply themselves to the obscure and recondite ; but as the vulgar and easy is the foundation on which the rare and arduous is built, they fail even in attaining the object of their ambition, and remain with only a farrago of confused and ill-assorted notions. In all its phases, self-love is an enemy to philosophical progress ; and the history of philosophy is filled with the illusions of which it has been the source. On the one side it has led men to close their eyes against the most evident truths which were not in harmony with their adopted opinions. It is said there was not a physician in Europe, above the age of forty, who would admit Harvey's discovery of the circulation of the blood. On the other hand, it is finely observed by Bacon, that 'the eye of the human intellect is not dry, but receives a suffusion from the will and the affections,' so that it may almost be said to engender any science it pleases. Let men throw off their old prejudices, and come with hearts willing to receive knowledge, and understandings open to conviction. Unless ' ye become as little children, ye shall not enter the kingdom of heaven.' Such is true religion ; such, also, is true philosophy. Philosophy requires an emancipation from the yoke of foreign authority, a renunciation of all blind adhesion to the opinions of our age and country, and a purification of the intellect from all assumptive beliefs. Unless we can cast off the prejudices of the man, and become as children, docile and unperverted, we need never hope to enter the temple of philosophy. It is the neglect of this primary condition which has mainly occasioned men to wander from *the unity of truth*, and caused the endless variety of religious and philosophical sects."

The unity of truth, the correlation of inherent ideas, the harmonious correspondence and fixed relationships of things, constitute the central charm of all intellectual effort and research. It is both consoling and exalting to know, for example, that the MATTER of the living organizations of the universe is identical (that is, the *same* in essence as that) with which the inorganic forms of the world are constituted. This truth brings all things together. And it is indispensable to our philosophy of the Summer Land. It shows that the forces in your organs are the same as the forces—gravitational, chemical, mechanical, electrical, spiritual. With Prof. Huxley, you logically come to the broad conclusion that " not only as to living matter itself, but as to the forces

that matter exerts, there is a close relationship between
the organic and the inorganic world—the difference between them arising from the diverse combination and
disposition of identical forces, and not from any
primary diversity, as far as we can see."

In examining the relations subsisting between man's
senses, we find that the universe may be conceived as
" a polygon of a thousand or a hundred thousand sides
or facets—and each of these sides or facets may be conceived as representing one special mode of existence.
Now, of these thousand sides or modes all may be
equally essential, but three or four only may be turned
toward us, or be analogous to our organs. One side or
facet of the universe, as holding a relation to the organ
of sight, is the mode of luminous or visible existence;
another, as proportional to the organ of hearing, is the
mode of sonorous or audible existence; and so on. But
if every eye to see, if every ear to hear, were annihilated,
the modes of existence to which these organs now stand
in relation—that which could be seen, that which could
be heard—would still remain; and if the intelligences,
reduced to the three senses of touch, smell, and taste,
were then to assert the impossibility of any modes of
being except those to which these three senses were
analogous, the procedure would not be more unwar-
ranted, than if we now ventured to deny the possible
reality of other modes of material existence than those
to the perception of which our five senses are accommodated."

In this volume we must fortify our positions, relative
to the substantiality of the Summer Land, by laying a
broad foundation in the principles and facts of science.

Hence my impressions carry me directly into the con-current testimony of living philosophers and scientific men. If I were to present exclusively my own interior perceptions, and leave unnoticed all the important cor-roborations of positive science, the world would discard the whole as mere "speculation."

Hence now I refer you to a physiological authority: " All things which are in the brain of man are arranged into series, and, as it were, into fascicles; and into series within series, thus into fascicles. That such an arrangement has place, is evident from the arrange-ment of all things in the body, where fibers appear arranged into fascicles, and little glands into collections of glands, and this in the body throughout; still more perfectly in the purer parts which are not discernible by the naked eye; this fasciculation is principally pre-sented to view *in the brain*, in the two substances there, one of which is called cortical, and the other medullary; the case is not unlike in the purer principles, and at length in the most pure, where the forms which receive them are the very forms of life; that forms or substances are recipients of life, may be manifest from the singular things which appear in the living; also that recipient forms or substances are arranged in a manner the most suitable for influx of life; without the reception of life in substances, which are forms, there would not be given any living thing in the natural world, nor in the spiritual world; series of the most pure stamina, like fascicles, are what constitute those forms. . . . . As the External acts or is acted upon, so the Internals also act or are acted upon, for there is a perpetual confasciculation of the whole. For

example, take in the body some common covering, as
the pleura, which is the common covering of the breast,
or of the heart and lungs, and examine it with an ana-
tomical eye, or, if you have not made this your particular study, consult anatomists, and they will tell you
that this common covering, by various circumvolutions,
and afterward by exsertions or derivations from itself,
finer and finer, enters into the *inmost* substance of the
lungs, even to the smallest bronchial ramifications, and
into the follicles themselves, which are the beginnings
of the lungs : Not to mention its progression afterward
by the trachea to the larynx toward the tongue ; from
which it is evident that there is a perpetual connection
of the Outmost with the Inmost, wherefore as the Outmost acts or is acted upon, so also the Interiors from
the Inmost or Intimates act or are acted upon."

Physiologists, as a class, are not seers of the spiritual
within the natural. They observe organs, study functions,
trace the nerve-connections throughout the economy,
but seldom go deeper. But those who *do* probe below
the apparent, who explore the interior mansions of the
temple, find exactly what is embodied in the foregoing
testimony. As the chemist finds elements within elements, as meteorologists find atmospheres within atmospheres, as geologists find strata within strata, as
botanists find leaf within leaf and flower within flower,
so physiologists find organs within organs, and inde-
scribably finer determinations of vital power within the
familiar forces of the human body. There is, too,
everywhere manifested a law from the infinite magazine
of principles, called the "centripetal force," whereby
every thing is cohesively and affectionately clasped to

the central Heart. And every thing would forever play and roll around the all-loving centripetal affections of the spiritual universe, were it not for the inherent principle of Justice, the mother of all distributions and the father of all equilibriums, whereby every thing is taken in the giant arms of omnipotent "centrifugal force," and is by that masculine force sent abroad through the illimitable immensities, and commanded to "take plenty of out-door exercise, eat all they can honestly get, rest when weary, and earn their own living." And so the laws and the essences go from the warm home of centripetal attraction, become acquainted, and conjugate together, so that, like Adam and Eve, they may multiply and replenish the universe. On this middle ground, in the meeting and mating and prolification of laws and essences, we behold the marriage of Mind with Matter, and can, if we will, trace out the generations which proceed from them—in the diversified forms and forces of the world without.

"Laws" are the most *descended* modification of the central Mind; whilst "essences" are the most *ascended* form and condition of Matter; and their marriage is followed by the instantaneous vivification of substance and the universal manifestation of forces, principles,. and ideas. But this marriage ceremony is occurring every moment; it eternally exists, as much behind as future; and yet, owing to the limitations of thought, man must "begin" his reasonings and "end" with conclusions—the process being true and strictly logical, also, so far as it refers scientifically to *one* cycle of development in the universal whole.

By the marriage of Laws with Essences, we obtain,

on the one side, all the successive condescensions and condensations of Matter, and, on the other side, all the evolutions and manifestations of Mind. Conditions of Matter, once called "imponderable substances," float out of existence, leaving behind only vibrations or "agitations" of the one unchangeable reality termed Matter. The translator of Reichenbach's *Odic-Mag-netic Letters*, concerning his experiments in Odic-forces, has not failed to observe how perfectly that earnest philosopher's radiant demonstrations coincide with the deductions of inductive science. He recognizes the conceded maxim that there is no more nor no less matter now than there was fifty thousand years ago; there is no more and no less force. "Wave your hand," says Grove; "the motion has apparently ceased, but it is taken up by the air, from the air by the walls of the room, and so by direct and re-acting waves continually communicated, but never destroyed. Let us suppose that two balls rolling toward each other strike; the motion appears to be lost, but it changes to heat and electricity; to heat if the balls be homogeneous, and electricity if heterogeneous. If the balls be greased so that they will glance from each other, they will lose little motion and create little heat, precisely in proportion to the loss of one force is the development of others. And the motion or friction of the electrical machine develops electricity, electricity produces magnetism, light, heat, and motion, and influences chemical affinity, as is seen in the composition and decomposition of compound substances. Heat produces motion, and our thermometers are constructed to measure heat by the expansion or motion which it causes in certain sub-

7

stances. Heat also develops electricity. An evidence of this may be obtained by heating bars of bismuth and antimony, the ends of which are in contact. Unite the other ends by an iron wire, and an electric current will pass over it and heat the wire. The relationship of light to heat is very near, and they closely resemble each other in their phenomena. Both are radiated in direct lines, reflected, refracted, doubly refracted, and polarized. Heat also influences chemical affinity.

"Light influences chemical action, which latter develops electricity, and that, magnetism, heat, and motion. A coil of wire, attached to a daguerreotype plate, becomes electric when the plate is exposed to the light. Pieces of cloth, of different colors, sink with different speed into snow, showing that the light, when absorbed by black cloths, changes into heat, and therefore these cloths sink more rapidly into the snow.

"As electricity, moving round an iron bar, develops magnetism, so revolving magnets develop electricity, and we have magneto-electricity as well as electro-magnetism. Since electricity causes light, heat-motion, and chemical affinity, magnetism may be considered to cause them. Magnets directly cause and resist motion; and whenever iron is magnetized or demagnetized, heat is developed.

"Chemism, the power which causes chemical action, by means of chemical affinity, causes motion, electricity, heat, and light. All these effects are seen in the chemical process of burning; one of our strongest sources of electricity is in chemical action; and in the Voltaic-pile and Galvanic battery, the amount of electricity evolved is in exact proportion to the amount of chemical action ; in the same way as the heat and electricity caused by friction are in exact proportion to the amount of the friction and to the loss of mechanical force. It is believed that the vital forces are also connected with the physical forces of inanimate nature. All the substances found in the animal are also found in the mineral kingdom. And light and heat are necessary conditions to animation."

THE SUMMER LAND ZONE WITHIN THE MILKY WAY,

"If I have told you of earthly things, and ye believe not, how shall ye believe if I tell you of heavenly things?"—*Testimony of Mary's Son, as recorded in the New Testament.*

CHAPTER XII.

THE CONSTITUTION OF THE SUMMER-LAND.

Thus far we have cautiously walked in the fact-lighted path of inductive science. We are, nevertheless, in search of that attractive Spiritual Zone—which blends, astronomically and mathematically, the finite with the infinite—to which the human heart and the cultured mind instinctively aspire. We are intellectually searching for that higher Land which, accepting the testimony of seers, rolls embosomed in the Stellar Universe. In looking through the boundless blue for our eternal home, we behold, as by necessity, the holy orbs and sun-built constellation of the ethereal realm.

> "Ye stars! which are the poetry of heaven,
>   If in your bright leaves we would read the fate
> Of men and empires—'tis to be forgiven;
>   *   *   *   For ye are
> A beauty and a mystery, and create
>   In us such love and reverence from afar
> That fortune, fame, power, life, have named themselves a star."

Chemistry has many living exponents, and they all agree that the sixty-four or eighty-two "simple elements," by entering into different atomic arrangements, and by combining in different proportions, originate all the known "compounds" and organizations in nature.

It is according to my perceptions, however, that chemists, when better informed, will resign their now popular theory of " Simples." The number and names of the " primates" are increased each succeeding year by the discovery of several new elements. An element, in the chemical schools, is understood to be that which cannot be further analyzed or changed in its nature. Gold, for example, can be vaporized so finely as to become invisible ; but when detected, accumulated, and assayed, each grain of it is exactly and perfectly what it was at first. There is no intrinsic difference between the finest grain and the largest mass, and thus gold is called an " element."

But the magnificent simplicities of Nature, like the central unities of Truth, when they are detected and correctly assayed, will put an everlasting extinguisher upon all these false " lights" in the temple of chemical science. It will be found that the solids of the world came from ethers and essences. The atmospheres contain in solution all the world. (In this work I do not use the terms " fluids " and " vapors " in any ordinary limited sense.) It is certain to a demonstration that *essences* are the magnetical condition of matter. The different electricities exist in the sphere below, among the " vapors;" as the atmospheres, and the so-called gases, exist in the " fluids " of earth and space. It is necessary to understand this, before your judgment can take in the conception of a stratified spiritual Zone, because the celestial existence is constituted of the ultimate atoms of visible matter. And it is, therefore, of the highest moment, scientifically considered, that the *essence-origin* of palpable solid matter be perfectly comprehended. For if it be clearly seen that the earth was once impalpable ether or essence, and if the established world-forming laws and processes of space be remembered, as we have carefully explained them in earlier chapters, then it will be logically easy to understand the formation and constitution of the Summer Land.

The ethereal condition, or, rather, the *essence-origin of visible matter*, therefore, is the question first to be considered. On this point, then, we must take testimony accumulated by the world's chemical researches. An English writer, full of positivism and skepticism, *first* asks a question and then answers, thus:—

" *What is man ?* (and this term equally applies chemically to the whole organic world.) Man is a condensation of gases and vapors, every one of which are floating round us in the atmosphere. Out of his total weight of 154 lbs., we have in the man—oxygen, 111 lbs., and he is inhaling it every instant; hydrogen, 15 lbs., a gas we burn; carbon, a gas, when combined with oxygen; nitrogen, part of the air we breathe; phosphorus, which is all around us in every plant and animal, which we eat at every meal; calcium, liquid in water; sodium, liquid with chlorine; and other metals in very small quantities, all susceptible of liquidity. Man is not conscious of it, any more than he is conscious that when he is eating roast-beef, he is eating nitrogen, phosphorus, calcium, sulphur, potassium, and iron; few even are conscious that, in taking salt, they are eating chlorine. Man is continually giving out these vapors, which are in fact a part of himself; he is conscious only of one thing, and that is, that if they escape a little too fast, he feels cold. The quantity of these vapors is immense. The runaway negro leaves his track distinguishable by the blood-hound for 100 miles—we scarcely perceive it, but if a dog has lost his master, he knows if his master has been in any room he goes into ; such is the absolutely distinctive difference of the emanations from each individual. These emanations are as positively material, as the individual himself is material—as material as, if you scent a large room with one drop of otto of roses, every particle by which you perceive the scent is as material as the whole drop itself was. Now these emanations correspond exactly with Baron Reichenbach's description, in his conclusions of Odyle, p. 210, namely :—

A peculiar force, distinct from all known forces, is different from magnetism.

Bodies possessing it do not assume any particular direction from the earth's magnetism.

In animals, at least in man, the whole left side is in odylic opposition to the right. The force appears concentrated on poles in the extremities; the hands and fingers, in both feet, stronger in the hands than in the feet.

The odylic force is conducted to distances yet unascertained by all solid and liquid bodies; not only metals, but glass, resin, silk, water, dry wood, paper, cotton cloth, woolen cloth, &c.

Bodies may be charged with odyle, or odyle may be transferred from one body to another. In stricter language, a body in which free odyle is developed can excite in another body a similar odylic state.

This charging, or transference, is effected by contact.

The charging requires a certain time, and is not accomplished under several minutes.

The odylic light of amorphous bodies is a kind of feeble external and internal glow, somewhat similar to phosphorescence. This glow is surrounded by a delicate luminous vail, in the form of a fine downy flame.

Human beings are thus luminous over nearly the whole surface, but especially the hands, over the palm of the hand, the points of the fingers, the eyes, certain parts of the head, the pit of the stomach, the toes, &c.

Flaming emanations stream forth from all the points of the fingers, of relatively great intensity, and in the line of the length of the fingers.

All these flames may be moved by currents of air; and where they meet with solid bodies, they bend round them, just as ordinary flame does. The odylic flame has therefore an obviously material (ponderable?) character.

In the animal economy, night, sleep, and hunger depress and diminish the odylic influence. Taking food, daylight, and the active waking state, increase and intensify it. In sleep the seat of odylic activity is transferred to other parts of the nervous system.

A photographic picture is the electric effect of light —the action of electricity on metals. But man is a compound of the very materials used in photography, only in solution. You have sodium, a white metal; calcium, a white metal; iodine, chlorine, and particularly phosphorus, and you have a continued internal spring of electricity. It is curious also that any excess or diminution of phosphorus in the brain affects the sense and imagination.

7*

"In a work I have before me," says this author, "it is stated that the analysis of the brain of man and animals gives the following proportions of phosphorus:—

In animals of the lower order......................	1	per cent.
In imbeciles (men)...............................	1½	"
In men of sound intellectual powers.................	2 to 2½	"
In men where a degree of eccentricity prevailed	3	"
Complete insanity...............................	4 to 4½	"

Phosphorus is a substance in a great measure composed of light. I wish you first to reflect on the intimate connection of the light with thought, so that the state of the intellectual faculties seems to be regulated by it; and next, that these varying quantities are only the result of the different power of the absorbents of different individuals.

"In Mons. Boinet's work on Iodotherapia, we find that Mons. Chaton states that the absence of iodine in the air, in certain countries, is the cause of the degradation of the human species. Further—the researches and observations of Messrs. Boussingault, Gange, Cantu, and a number of scientific men, prove that in those geographical, geological, and chemical situations where iodine is deficient, cretinism or imbecility abounds. This points strongly to iodine as having properties related to intellect—and salt, in which the metal sodium is but the vehicle for chlorine, what would the world be without it? The most noticeable facts in the case are—the large quantity of phosphorus in every human body—1¾lb.; the fact that we imbibe phosphorus in each bit of animal and vegetable food we eat; that the lower the animal kingdom is in intellect or instinct, the less phosphorus their bodies contain; and that the odylic emanations and intelligent manifestations are generally and most probably always accompanied by phosphorus; and that chlorine, which we are always eating in salt, being a sister element to iodine, is full as likely as iodine to have a part in the development of intellect."

The materialism of this testimony does no injury to the purpose in view, namely, to adduce scientific facts to establish the essence-origin of matter. Innumerable atomic emanations arise and continually ascend from the bodies of persons composing the human family; not less than 800,000,000 tons per annum; atoms that float out into space in the rivers of ether, and enter into the constitution of the Summer Land. This process has been long known to seers. But the world's people want "facts" of the schools for the foundation of their faith in the future. "Life, in its proper, generic sense," says Grindon, in his volume on the Varieties and Phenomena of Life, "is the name of the sustaining principle by which every thing out of the Creator subsists, whether worlds, metals, minerals, trees, animals, mankind, angels, or devils, together with all thought and feeling. Nothing is absolutely lifeless, though many things are relatively so; and it is simply a conventional restriction of the term, which makes life signify no more than the vital energy of an organized material body.

"Has not this inorganic nature sympathies and antipathies in those mysterious elective affinities of the molecules of matter which chemistry investigates? Has it not the powerful attractions of bodies to each other, which govern the motions of the stars scattered in the immensity of space, and keep them in an admirable harmony? Do we not see, and always with a secret astonishment, the magnetic needle agitated at the approach of a particle of iron, and leaping under the fire of the Northern Light? Place any material body whatever by the side of another, do they not immediately enter into relations of interchange, of molecular attraction, of electricity, of magnetism? In the inorganic part of matter, as in the organic, all is acting, all is promoting change, all is itself undergoing transformation. And thus, though this life of the globe, this physiology of our planet, is not the life of the tree or the bird, is it not *also* a life? Assuredly it is. We cannot refuse so to call those lively actions and reactions, that perpetual play of the forces of matter, of which we are every day the witnesses. . . .

" Thus, that the soul is no 'will-o'-th'-wisp in the swamps of the cerebrum,' but an *internal man*, a body within a body; 'a life,' as Aretæus says of the womb, ' within a life;' in the material body as God is in the universe, everywhere and nowhere; everywhere for the enlightened intellect, nowhere for the physical view; no more in the brain than in the toes, but the spiritual 'double' of the entire fabric. All the organs of the material body have soul in them, and serve the soul, each one according to its capacity; yet is the soul itself independent of them all, because made of another substance. . . . .

" Spiritual substances are none the less real because out of the reach of chemistry or edgetools, or because they are inappreciable by the organs of sense. Indeed it is only the grosser expressions of matter which can be so treated, and which the senses can apprehend. Heat and electricity are as truly material as flint and granite, yet man can neither cut, nor weigh, nor measure them; while the most familiar and abundant expression of all, the air which we breathe, can neither be seen nor felt till put in motion. As for invisibility, which to the vulgar is proof of non-existence, no warning is so incessantly addressed to us, from every department of creation, as not to commit the mistake of disbelieving, simply because we cannot see. Each class of substances is real in relation to the world it belongs to ; material substances in the material world ; spiritual substances in the spiritual world ; and each kind has to be judged of according to its place of abode."

The testimony of science is stronger and stronger in favor of the essence-origin of all forms and conditions of matter; and how much more satisfactory to the externalist, to the sensuous thinker, that this testimony proceeds from recognized literary and scientific authority. The venerable philosopher, Dr. Ashburner, of England, gives most important evidence that matter can be "dissolved" and "attenuated" *beyond* the influence of "attraction." The unparticled atomic constitution of the Summer Land, therefore, is an acknowledged possibility. That philosopher and scientist says: "It is idle to discuss the various characteristics of the forms of the objects surrounding us. Those who have the necessary faculties are quite aware that all the objects in nature are resolvable into certain forms known as solid, liquid, and gaseous or aëriform. We have, on a previous occasion, illustrated a portion of our present subject by selecting the lightest substance known as material, hydrogen gas, in order to express our meaning of infinitely attenuated matter, when a repulsive force operates to keep its particles asunder so as to prevent its combining with any other form of matter. The force of repulsion, then, obliges hydrogen to remain in a state of negative polarity; for unless its particles can be approximated, it cannot alter its state or its conditions. Nor can any matter without the intervention of force, for all matter is known to be inert or passive. If man be operating on matter, in any course of experiments, it would be idle to say that he was not exerting his will to fashion those experiments. It has been shewn that the will of man is a force, attractive or repulsive, according to circumstances. [See his Essays in the fourth volume of the *Zoist*.] Man can cause matter to be dissolved. It can be dissolved as a salt in water, which is itself a form of matter, capable of expansion and attenuation in the form of vapor or gas. But in order to effect this change in water, the introduction of a repulsive force is necessary. Under all circumstances, matter is subject to force. Cannot force dissolve matter? What do we mean by electro-metallurgy? Does not, in this case, electricity dissolve metal? In the formation of vapor in the atmosphere, does not force dissolve water? Is not all attenuation of matter more or less a solution in force?

" This idea, expanded, takes us on to that of infinite space. We can suppose all matter to be so far attenuated as to *form universal ether ;* to be dissolved by force in infinite space; resolved into such minute particles, as to be no longer subject to attraction."

In this place it is of the first importance to read a

communication that appeared in the London (England) *Spiritual Magazine* concerning the *essences* and *ethers* and *emanations* which science has discovered as belonging to and proceeding from physical bodies. The correspondent, after alluding appreciatively to the letters of Mr. Ruskin, says:—

" It is to one of his physical illustrations that we wish to draw our reader's attention. It is one of the demonstrations of spiritual clairvoyance that each of us is surrounded by a spiritual sphere or emanation; which is sometimes even seen in colors, or in light, and is more often absolutely felt, even through our dulled and deadened sensibilities. Nothing, indeed, is more likely to be true, or can be more profusely illustrated by our experience, than the impression by thoughts or by pre-monitions on meeting persons of our acquaintance, or in many of the circumstances of our daily lives, and intercourse with one another; but, like most that is spiritual, and appertaining to the soul and its faculties, it is received with ridicule or neglect. We look forward, however, to a future day when it will be a key-stone in the arch of spiritual knowledge.

" The discovery of the spectrum analysis, which now plays so important a part in physical science, and is being prosecuted in so many quarters of physics, is now helping us, by demonstrating similar spheres and emanations in natural substances. This also has long ago been described and insisted on by Spiritualists, but their testimony has been disregarded. A very interesting description is given of the recent discoveries or rather re-discoveries on the physical plane, made through a friend of Mr. Ruskin, and which he thus narrates:—

" 'Yesterday afternoon I called on Mr. H. C. Sorby, to see some of the results of an inquiry he has been following all last year, into the nature of the coloring matter of leaves and flowers. You most probably have heard (at all events, may with little trouble hear) of the marvelous power which chemical analysis has received in recent discoveries respecting the laws of light. My friend showed me the rainbow of the rose, and the rainbow of the violet, and the rainbow of the hyacinth, and the rainbow of forest leaves being born, and the rainbow of forest leaves dying. And, last, he showed me the rainbow of blood. It was but the three-hundredth part of a grain, dissolved in a drop of water; and it cast its measured bars, forever recognizable now to human sight, on the chord of the seven colors. And no drop of that red rain can now be shed, so small as that the stain of it cannot be known, and the voice of it heard out of the ground.'

"Shall there be," he inquires, "a rainbow or sphere around the rose, or around a drop of blood, and no emanation from the soul, with all its God-given powers, and its undying loves, and heavenward aspirations? The natural is but the analogue of the spiritual; and poetry is true, though science, till now, has failed to see it."

The reader will, possibly, find that the deepest truths are vailed in obscurity. Many of our plainest principles form a kind of *mysterium magnum*—immensely incomprehensible—arising in part, perhaps wholly, from the inadequacy of language to convey clear pictures and images of Ideas to the mind. Indeed, it must forever remain difficult to impart to the mind of another a perfectly crystalline conception and knowledge of things spiritual. The faithful, truthful logical thinker knows that the visible world is but a vail, a material garment, transparent to the spirit's eyes, hiding from physical vision the formative powers which are eternal. The material constitution and substantialness of the Summer Land become a "matter of fact" to that mind which is structurally endowed and unfolded by culture to discern the harmonious essences that perpetually build up the temple of the universe, and which can

> —— "look through natural forms,
> And *feel* the throbbing arteries of LAW
> In every pulse of Nature and of Man."

Thus far, in this section of our subject, I have led the reader through the fields of "scientific facts." And to this method, for a time longer, I am constrained to adhere ; because the materialized millions of America demand, even from me, the plain evidences of intellectual and passionless science.

Before us now, therefore, is the labor of establishing in your mind *two* grand truths : namely, first, that the so-called "solid" matter of the universe is continually *rising* to its ultimate condition (which is the reproduction of its primitive condition), but in a far higher circle of refinement, called "essences ;" and, second, that from the human organization, especially, these "essences" are continually emanating and sweeping off into space, being the *highest* emanations of refined matter from any globe, because the human body is the highest organism, and is pre-eminently one of "God's mills" for preparing atoms to enter into the formation of the velvety soils in the successive Summer Lands of immensity.

The first time I clairvoyantly saw the "second

sphere "—*i. e.* the nearest Summer Land, lining this part
of the stellar universe—it seemed only as a small section of a continuous *white* zone among the stars. The
little diagram gives a hint of its first appearance in
space.

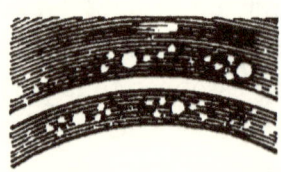

Let the reader imagine my amazement and delight, succeeded by an unutterable *awe,* arising from the unpre-
paredness of my intellect for such a disclosure. Although
I have since seen a million times more vast and wonderful things, concerning the spiritual and celestial universes, yet the mere recalling of that *first* impression
and perception, which occurred almost a quarter of a
century ago, thrills my mind through and through.
The universe is ablaze every moment with these myriad-
gated spheres of beauty and glory. The infinite-master
Powers of the Univercœlum, and the plastic Essences
and animated Ethers of the highest regions of Matter,
and the grand white Light of the innermost empyrean,
are all beautifully and philosophically disclosed to that
mind which is intelligently and worthily *open* to the
perception and comprehension of God's choicest truths.
The vast panorama of the Universe, in its epical
grandeur and lyrical harmonies, should be pictured
as true and pure as frost-flowers upon your reason.
The intellect of that man who beholds these lofty
truths is supremely blest. Henceforth he should hold
his—

"— gift in reverence. And he should mold his life
In beauty's perfect fashion, holding on
Columbus-like through floods of thought unknown,
Till tropic archipelagoes of song,
Till virgin continents of stately verse,
And undiscovered worlds of harmony
Repay the bold adventure."

Such a philosopher, standing armed to the teeth with the facts of positive science, would be constrained to testify that when " we look on a beautiful landscape, we see mountains, trees, rivers, real and substantial as regards the material universe; nevertheless, only as images, forms originally existing, in a world which we do *not* see, and from which they are derived . . forms which are as real as the material—yea, infinitely more so, since the material is local and temporary, whereas the spiritual is unlimited and imperishable. Nothing exists except by reason of the spiritual world ; whatever pertains to the material is purely and simply effect."

According to my most careful examinations of the physical structure of the Summer Land, the fertile soils, and the lovely groves and vines and flowers which infinitely diversify the landscape, are *constituted of particles that were once in human bodies!* But the world-rearing principles, by which those particles were attracted from the human emanations of all the inhabited planets in the solar belt called the Milky Way, are from the spiritual universe. These human emanations, like the lights and flames of crystals and magnets, flow forth unceasingly, in millions of tons daily, into the soils of the celestial lands.

Perhaps it may fortify your judgment to read Reichenbach's testimony. His experiments with "sensitives," as he terms the neurological mediums of Germany, demonstrate that "every flower, fruit, and tree emits into nature the best portion of its being—its essence." But who has seen the aromal essence of a flower? Who has beheld the essential form thus given off into the universe?*

According to the Teutonic philosopher, the odic light is more beautiful from the horseshoe magnet, set upright, with both poles pointing toward the heavens. "I have," he writes in one of his letters, "a nine-leaved horseshoe magnet, with a power of raising a hundred pounds; and all sensitive persons can see a fine light streaming out of each pole—that is, two lights side by side, which do not attract, nor influence, nor extinguish each other—as do the magnetic forces of opposing poles—but steadily stream up high, side by side, and form a light-column, as large as a man, and composed of innumerable light-sparkles in constant motion—the column being described as impressively beautiful by all who have seen it. It rises perpendicularly to the ceiling, and there casts a light upon a space about twelve feet in diameter. If the magnet is kept long in this position before the sensitive person, the whole ceiling becomes gradually visible. Such a magnet upon a table throws a light upon it, so that every thing on its surface can be seen for a yard in each direction from the magnet. A hand interposed between the flame and the table casts a perceptible shadow. If you hold a piece of board, a pane of window-glass, a plate of tin, or any

---

* These emanations have been seen by many clairvoyants. For the author's perception of them, read a chapter in "The Seer" (Harmonia, vol. IIL); also see a chapter in "The Magic Staff."

similar body horizontally into the flame, the latter will
bend under it and rise up at the sides, just as the flame
of a fire would under the same circumstances. If a
draft of air blow upon the magnet, or if it be moved,
the flame bends to one side, as the flame of a candle
would. The light can be collected in a focus by a
burning-glass, like the rays of ordinary light. The
phenomenon is thus shown to be a material one, and
has many qualities in common with ordinary flame. If
two of these odic flames be made to cross each other,
there is no perceptible attraction or repulsion, but they
mutually pierce each other, and pursue their respective
courses undisturbed. If one be stronger than the other
—if its sparkles of light have a stronger headway—it
divides the weaker flame, which splits, passes over the
sides of the stronger one, and meets on the other side,
just as it does if a stick be held in it. And as sensitive
persons saw the crystals penetrated by a fine glow, so
also they see the steel magnet translucent with a
white light; and electro-magnets have the same
appearance."

That all the universe of matter is pervaded by an
invisible essence, is to be the grandest discovery of
chemical science. Cornelius Agrippa, in his great
works on Occult Philosophy, recognized the existence
of this sympathetic and antipathetic essence between
and throughout all things. This essence is not a mere
motion of matter in a high state of attenuation; it is,
in fact, a substantial form of matter itself; and we find
that the Summer Land derived its constitution from the
atoms composing this inter-stellar and inter-planetary
etherealized ocean of materials.

Now the laws that govern nature go on, as I have many times urged, with a steady and unchangeable progression. They are not at any time retarded or accelerated. Nothing can prevent the natural results of these laws. They are established by one great positive power and mind; and equaled and balanced by a negative or ultimate equilibrium. Hence their continued and united forces, by the influence of which all things are actuated, governed, and developed, pass on in a steady progression. Every particle of matter possesses the same power which governs the whole of the universe, and in each particle you see a representation and evidence of those divine laws. Thus, in the stone you may see the properties of the soil; in the soil, the properties of the plant; in the plant, the properties of an animal; in the animal you see man—and in Man you cannot *see*, but you can *feel* the immortal principle.

The testimony of years ago is as fresh and momentous now as then. I am equally desirous of enforcing that *great spiritual and eternal truth* which it is necessary for man to know and appreciate before he can comprehend the idea of the Summer Land ; and that is, *that all manifest substances, forms, compositions—indeed, that* ALL THINGS VISIBLE *are expressions of an interior productive cause, which is the spiritual essence ;* that the Mineral Kingdom is an expression of *Motion,* the Vegetable an expression of *Life,* the Animal an expression of *Sensation,* and that Man is an expression of *Intelligence ;* that the planets in our solar system are a perfect expression of the Sun, from which they sprang ; that the various combined bodies and planetary systems in the Universe

are a perfect expression of the Great Sun of the Univercœlum; that the Great Sun is the perfect expression of
the SPIRITUAL SUN within it; and that the Spiritual
Sun is a perfect expression of the Divine Mind, Love,
or Essence. The Spiritual Sun is thus the Center and
Cause of all material things. It is a diverging or radiating Sphere or Atmosphere of the Great Eternal Cause.
It is an *aroma*—a garment and a perfect radiation of
the more interior Essence, the Divine, Creative Soul.

Some conception of the Stellar Universe (*i. e.*, the
universe of suns and planets) may be obtained from a
synoptical sketch of astronomic discoveries. Prof.
Meigs reports M. Arago's lecture to this effect:—We
count in the Northern Hemisphere 4,400 stars visible
to the naked eye. And for the purpose of counting we
proceed in this way: through a narrow slit, corresponding with the meridian of the place of observation,
we look attentively and note the stars gradually as
they appear. The following approximate calculation
will give an inferior limit to the number of stars visible
with the powerful instruments of which we have the
use.

Observation has demonstrated that the number of
the stars of the *second* magnitude *is triple* that of
those of the *first* magnitude; that those of the *third*
magnitude is *triple* that of those of the *second* magnitude. In a word, that in general to obtain the number
of stars of any given magnitude, we must multiply by
three the number of stars of a preceding magnitude.

Let us, then, admit this law to the 14th magnitude—
to stars which the most powerful instruments render
visible; as the number of stars of the first magnitude is

eighteen, then the number of stars visible by the naked eye and with telescopes as far as the 14th magnitude will be about *twenty-nine millions;* and if to these twenty-nine millions we add those of the 13th and 14th magnitudes, &c., we obtain the number of *forty-three millions of stars.*

Herschel, in that part of the heavens occupied by the knee of Orion, in a band of fifteen degrees long by two degrees wide, has distinctly counted *fifty thousand stars.* And as the band is only the three hundred and seventy-sixth part of the celestial vault, the entire surface of the heavens must contain 98,755,000 visible with the telescope. And as we must remark, in a great many regions of the heavens the stars are much closer together, and that with our telescopes we only reach the least distant celestial spaces and the stars least remote, we must recognize the fact that the first estimate of their numbers is infinitely far from the truth; and that, admitting one visible star in each square minute, we must have a number of distinct stars amounting to one hundred and forty-eight millions five hundred and seven thousand two hundred stars, and yet remain much below the truth. There are then one hundred and forty-eight millions of stars, and *our sun is one of them* only. The mass of our earth is but the three hundred and fifty-five millionth part of that one sun; and we are but an atom in relation to our earth. The place we occupy is then infinitely small, and *we more than infinitely little.*

COMPARATIVE INTENSITIES OF THE LIGHT OF STARS OF DIFFERENT MAGNITUDES.—There is in science a great and much to be regretted blank; photometry, or the art of measuring the various intensities of light, is still in its infancy; we have hardly taken the first step.

The division of the stars by the order of their magnitude was made by the astronomers of antiquity in an arbitrary manner and without any pretension to exactness, and this vagueness is continued in our modern charts. Those which are accredited now present a total table of eighteen stars of the first magnitude for the two hemispheres. Why eighteen, and not nineteen or twenty?

The stars of the first magnitude are far from having all the same intensity. The sixth order composed among the ancients the last visible to the naked eye; and in our day those of the seventh magnitude constitute the demarcation between the stars visible to the naked eye and the telescopic stars.

We may affirm that there are certainly stars in the firmament whose distance from the earth is 344 and even 900 times greater than that of the stars visible to the naked eye. See what conclusion this leads us to! It is admitted that light, with the velocity of 77,000 leagues a second, takes three years to reach us from the nearest star. And there are stars three hundred and forty-four and even nine hundred times more remote. Then there are stars whose light does not reach us until after two thousand seven hundred years—an infinity in distance as it is in numbers.

STARS OF VARIABLE INTENSITY OF LIGHT.--Eratosthenes, in the year 275 before Christ, says of the stars in the constellation of the Scorpion: "They are preceded by the most beautiful of all the northern gems." At this time this is less brilliant than the southern, and, above

6

all, than Arcturus. Then there have been changes since the time of Eratosthenes.

When Newton pronounced the sublime words, *universal attraction*, there was an outcry at its novelty ; it was a neologism ; it had occult qualities, &c. Now the words fill the world, of which they are its greatest reality.

DIAMETERS OF THE STARS.—Great diversity of opinion exists on this point. If we should take for their discs such as they appear to the naked eye, certain stars would be nine thousand millions of leagues in diameter —equal to twenty-seven thousand times greater diameter than the sun—and the most moderate calculations would be one thousand seven hundred millions. Herschel's last calculation was that *Arcturus* had a diameter of nearly four millions of leagues (twelve millions of miles). If the apparent diameter of two seconds and a half, assigned by Herschel to the *Goat*, was real, the mass of that star must be more than fourteen million times greater than that of our sun. But there is no certainty in this, nor any thing to question that our sun is a star.

The sublime idea that the Creator hath made all with number, weight, and measure, is followed by Plato, who called it the geometry of the heavens. Halley, the friend of Newton, believed that all the stars were of the same magnitude—that of our sun— and that difference of distance only caused the apparent difference of size.

NUMBER OF STARS.—The number visible by means of a telescope of twenty feet focal distance may be more than five hundred millions.

DISTANCE OF THE STARS OF SOME NEBULÆ.—We have supposed that the nebulæ of which we form part is not the largest of the three thousand nebulæ known to astronomers. Is it not very natural? Is it not as a million to one that it is so? When, therefore, on this hypothesis, and the facts stated by Herschel, that there are, at a medium, in the direction of our nebulæ, five hundred stars, that many nebulæ subtend an angle of ten minutes, and the very natural hypothesis that the distance between two consecutive stars among the five hundred is the distance of the earth from the nearest star, we must arrive at the conclusion that there are planets so distant from us that light, moving at the velocity of more than seventy-seven thousand leagues in a second of time, would take more than a million of years to reach us! These few words are enough to prove, as it seems to me, that we must admit our imaginations overwhelmed at the infinite number and distances in question.

The existence and essential constitution of the Summer Land must cease to excite skepticism in that intellect which contemplates the glory, the stupendous immensity, and the musical harmony of the stellar system. It is a grand demonstration and affirmation of science that light travels about 213,000 miles in a second! From the moon it takes five quarters of a second to come to us; from the sun, eight minutes; from Uranus, more than five hours; from the nearest fixed stars, three years; from a star of the seventh magnitude, 180 years; from one of the twelfth magnitude, 4,000 years; and from those yet more distant orbs, seen only through the best telescopes—Lord Rosse's, for instance—the light requires many tens of thousands of years to reach our planet.

Consequently, when we look at any of these bodies we do not see it as it is at present, but as it was at some former time more or less remote. We see the moon as it was some five quarters of a second ago; Jupiter, as it was fifty-two minutes ago; the nearest of the fixed stars, as it was three years ago; one of the twelfth magnitude, as it was 4,000 years ago; and so on.

New stars may have existed for thousands of years, comparatively near the confines of our solar system, which have not yet become visible to us; and others which still shine in our firmament may have passed out of existence before the time fixed for Noah's flood.

These facts and conclusions are acknowledged and acted upon by astronomers. They are true, independently of any theory of optics; since it matters not whether light is a body that actually travels, or a mere electrical phenomenon or a "motion" of force, as some would have it. It is sufficient to know that it takes a complete second before a luminous body, 213,000 miles distant, becomes visible to us, and a proportionably longer interval in case of bodies farther on.

It is strange, however, that no one has hitherto thought of reversing this problem; for it follows as a matter of course from what has been said already, that an observer in the moon, looking toward the earth, does not see it as it is at the moment of observation, but as it was five quarters of a second before. An observer from the sun sees it as it was eight minutes before. From Uranus, the time between the reality and the perception by the eye is more than two hours. From the nearest fixed stars, the interval is three years. "An inhabitant of a star of the twelfth magnitude, if we imagine him with unlimited power of vision, contemplating the earth, sees it as it was 4,000 years ago; when Memphis was founded, and patriarch Abraham wandered upon its surface. Possibly, in some star still farther removed from us, an observer, equally gifted, would at this very moment have obtained a view of the earth 6,000 years ago, the creation of mankind, and further back to the primeval chaos; and so on to the remotest bounds of the habitable universe."

The following cut illustrates the appearance of the Summer Land in relation to the southern branch of the Milky Way :—

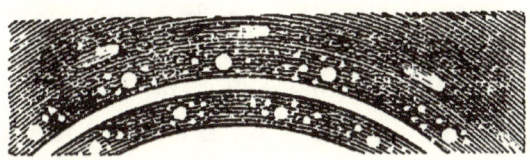

Thus astronomical science verges on the spiritual universe—yea, almost walks into "the house not made with hands"—whenever it goes abroad through the upper spheres searching for truth. Reasoning with the senses, to the unknown from what is visible, science is compelled substantially to say : " That the planets are inhabited by living animals, we have as positive evidence as we have that quadrupeds or even insects inhabit the yet unexplored islands of this earth; but whether they are inhabited by men or similar immortal beings is at present beyond the reach of human research. It is ascertained that these orbs, like our own, roll in regulated periods round the sun ; that they have nights and days, successions of seasons ; that they are provided with atmosphere supporting clouds and agitated by winds, and that thus, also, their climates and seasons are modified by evaporation, and that showers refresh their surfaces.

" For we know that wherever the existence of clouds is made manifest, there water must exist ; there evaporation must go on ; there electricity, with its train of phenomena, must reign ; there rains must fall ; there hail and snow descend.

" Notwithstanding the dense atmosphere and thick clouds with which Venus and Mercury are constantly enveloped, the telescope has exhibited to us great irregularities on their surfaces, and thus proved the existence of mountains and valleys. But it is upon the planet Mars, which approaches nearest to the earth, that the greatest advances have been made in this department of inquiry. Under favorable circumstances its disc is seen to be mapped out by varied outline, some portions being less reflective than land.

" Baer and Maedler, two Prussian astronomers, have devoted many years' labor to the examination of Mars; and the result has put us in possession of a map of the geography of that planet almost as exact and well-defined as that which we possess of our own. In fact, the geographical outlines of land and water have been made apparent upon it. But a still more extraordinary fact in relation to this planet remains to be considered. Among the shaded markings which have been noted by the telescope upon its disc, a remarkable region of brilliant white light, standing out in boldest relief, has been observed surrounding the visible pole. This highly illuminated spot is to be seen most plainly when it emerges from the long night of the winter season; but when it has passed slowly beneath the heat of the solar beams it is found to have gradually contracted its dimensions; and at last, before it has plunged into light on the opposite side, to have entirely disappeared. But the opposite pole, then coming into similar relations, is found to be furnished with a like luminous spot, which in its turn dissolves as it becomes heated by the summer sun.

"Now these facts prove to us incontestably, that the very geographical regions of Mars are fac-similes of our own. In its long polar winters, the snows accumulate in the desolation of its high northern and southern latitudes, until they become visible to us in consequence of their reflective properties; and these are slowly melted as the sun's rays gather power in the advancing season, until they cease to be appreciable to terrestrial eyes."

And yet over all, and through all, as much in the unnumbered littlenesses of the microscopic seas as in the boundlessness of the telescopic immensities, is the sweet consciousness of our never-ending life—the enshrined glory of our immortality. How impressively the poet Dana has set this feeling to the music of utterances:—

> "O listen, man!
> A voice within us speaks that startling word,
> 'Man! thou shalt never die!' Celestial voices
> Hymn it unto our souls; according harps
> By angel fingers touched, when the mild stars
> Of morning sang together, sound forth still
> The song of our great immortality.

Thick clustering orbs, and this our fair domain,
The tall dark mountains and the deep-toned seas,
Join in this solemn universal song.
O listen, ye, our spirits! drink it in
From all this air! 'Tis in the gentle moonlight;
'Tis floating midst Day's setting glories ; Night,
Wrapt in her sable robe, with silent step,
Comes to our bed, and breathes it in our ears.
Night and the Dawn, bright Day and thoughtful Eve :
All time, all bounds, the limitless expanse,
As one vast mystic instrument, are touched
By an unseen living hand, and conscious chords
Quiver with joy in this great jubilee.
——The dying hear it, and as sounds of earth
Grow dull and distant, wake their passing souls
To mingle in this heavenly harmony."

My present perceptions and understanding of the
atom-essence constitution of the Summer Land, and of
humanity's delicate spiritual relationships thereto, revive
beautiful memories of impressions imparted years ago.
And while observing the powerful movements of all
things contained in the terrestrial and celestial spheres,
there cannot but be a conception of Divine Wisdom
legitimately accompanying the former conclusion. The
innumerable centers of the stellar system; the many
suns, with their accompanying orbs, planets, and satellites ; the perfect precision of the general movements
of all these bodies ; their regular and connected adjustment and unity ; the distributive harmony and equilibrium of forces and motions which they constantly display—are all manifestations of grandeur, beauty, and
order unspeakable.   The regular inclination of orbits
and axes, and the definite distances of globes from each
other ; their constant sameness of motion and the uni-

form direction which all take; the apparent sympathy
and reciprocation of the spheres and atmospheres of the
innumerable and apparently independent bodies; the
united and constant action which each of these manifests
—all conspire to force upon the mind the irresistible
impression that the great and united movements of the
Universe are all being performed according to a most
inconceivably perfect adjustment of mathematical and
mechanical laws, and that all things are guided, in the
very motions of their inherent life and activity, by the
essence of Ómnipotent Wisdom! Their formation
and procreation; their particles and constituent parts
manifest, in their order and arrangement, the perfection
of pure Wisdom and Intelligence—while their numerical
extent, and diverse modes of development, infinitely
transcend the highest powers of human calculation and
demonstration. No process of analogical reasoning or
of mathematical calculation has reached that point of
perfection by which may be demonstrated and calculated the exact distances at which these spheres revolve,
the immensity of space which they occupy, and the
harmony of the whole!

All things are divine, both in the material and spiritual Universe; and all become celestial. So every
created spirit is invited by the progressive law of the
Father to its home; and when it enters, and becomes
sensible of the loveliness and purity thereof, it glorifies
the Father, not in prayer, but by *thought* and *deed* forever and ever. Each one, then, is an undying child of
the Eternal One, who is the Father of all; and no one
is so low but that it is the highest of some still lower,
and no one is so high but that it is the lowest of some

6*

yet undeveloped. One spirit cannot say unto another, "I need thee not;" for each one is the sustainer of another, and the mutual dependence constitutes the harmony and wisdom of all things.

CHAPTER XIII.

THE LOCATION OF THE SUMMER LAND.

UNDER this head a world of sublime realities press for immediate expression. For twenty years the clairvoyant perception and interior contemplation of the objective existence of the celestial world have been a source of unutterable joy. But I am admonished now, as I have been from the beginning of this Key, to supply, as far as possible, the testimony of different thinkers, seers, and speculators; so that, in the succeeding chapters of Part II. of this work, some clear and definite information may be both sought and imparted. The author's views, many of them, have already been published, but not with that scientific preciseness which may hereafter be demanded by close reasoners and the public generally. Now to the testimony.

In this place, and first of all, we introduce the evidence of a little boy, who, on his dying bed, and with his last breath, beheld and briefly described the Summer Land: The little child was dying. His weary limbs were racked with pain no more. The flush was fading from his thin cheeks, and the fever that for many days had been drying up his blood, was now cooling rapidly under the touch of the icy hand that was upon him.

There were sounds of bitter but suppressed grief in that dim chamber, for the dying little one was very

VIEW OF LAKE "MORNIA," IN THE SUMMER LAND.

The Egyptian Brotherhood is situated along the shores of the Silvery Sea; over which shine innumerable stars, the greatest and brightest of which is "Gunlarion."—MORNING LECTURES, p. 364. *et seq.*

dear to many hearts. They knew that he was departing, and the thought was hard to bear; but they tried
to command their feelings, that they might not disturb
the last moments of their darling.

The father and mother, and the kind physician, stood
beside dear Eddy's bed, and watched his heavy breathing. He had been silent for some time, and appeared
to sleep. They thought it might be thus that he would
pass away, but suddenly his mild blue eyes opened wide
and clear, and a beautiful smile broke over his features.
He looked upward and forward at first, and then, turn-
ing his eyes upon his mother's face, said, in a sweet
voice:

" Mother, what is the name of that beautiful country
that I see away beyond the mountains—the *high* mountains?"

"I can see nothing, my child," said the mother;
" there are no mountains in sight of our home."

" Look *there*, dear mother," said the child, pointing
upward; " *yonder* are the mountains. Can you not
see them *now?*" he asked, in tones of the greatest
astonishment, as his mother shook her head.

" They are so near me now—so large and high, and
behind them the country looks so beautiful, and the
people are so happy—*there are no sick children there.*
Papa, can you not see behind the mountains? Tell me
the name of that land!"

The parents glanced at each other, and with united
voice, replied:

"The Land you see is heaven, is it not, my child?"

" Yes, it is heaven. I thought that must be its name.
Oh, let me go—but how shall I cross those mountains?

Father, will you not carry me, for they call me from the other side, and I *must* go."

There was not a dry eye in that chamber, and upon every heart fell a solemn awe, as if the curtain which concealed its mysteries was about to be withdrawn.

"My son," said the father, "will you stay with us a little while longer? You shall cross the mountains soon, but in stronger arms than mine. Wait, stay with your mother a little longer; see how she weeps at the thought of losing you!"

"Oh, mother! oh, father! do not cry, but come with me, and cross the mountains—oh, come!" and thus he entreated, with a strength and earnestness which astonished all.

The chamber was filled with wondering and awe-stricken friends. At length he turned to his mother, with a face beaming with rapturous delight, and, stretching out his little arms to her for one last embrace, he cried: "Good-by, mother, I am going; but don't you be afraid—*the strong man has come to carry me over the mountains!*"

This impressive testimony is based upon the frequently demonstrated fact that the spiritual existence is revealed, with all its higher and most beautiful forms of beauty, to the refined and exalted sensibilities of old and young at the solemn moment of death. This proves also, that the divine law of growth and of spirit-perception is as operative in the least as in the greatest minds. Mind has been called "immaterial;" but it is as much material as any thing else. All things are really the same thing. Matter and soul, though said to be so different, actually consist of the same principle, though in different degrees of development. Soul is a more attenuated form of matter; this accounts for the imperceptibility of the soul by the physical eye. The eye can only discern things in the same sphere with itself, and those below. Hence the physical eye can only see physical things; while the spiritual eye can behold both spiritual and physical things. The physical eye is imperfect — the spiritual, perfect. The spiritual body is composed of matter which is refined and sublimated by the law of spiritual attraction.

In his reasonable and admirable volume — the "Arcana of Nature"—Hudson Tuttle affirms, with the force and assurance of an independent seer, that the realm of spirit-existence is as real, as tangible, and as consistent with human nature and natural laws, as is the globe on which we at present reside. "The second sphere," he affirms, "is a daguerreotype of earth. The refined matter which ascends is prone to assume the forms from which it was liberated on earth. The scenery is identical, but more beautiful and ethereal. Trees, fruits and flowers, are not individualized; that is, their emanations do not ascend to the spheres in an identified form, but their particles are more prone to assume such forms than any other. Thus the particles which exist in any particular flower in the spirit-world, have never existed in that plane before, but have ascended from a countless number of the same kind. The description of the splendid scenery we reserve for a future chapter. One thing only remains for us to elucidate. We speak of dwellings—of artificial things —as existing in the spirit-world. Are they created by our simply desiring them ?   So, many spirits have falsely taught.   It is true, our desires create them ; but we employ means, just as man does, to accomplish our wishes. We are not miniature gods, capable of creating a palace by a wish.   The marvelous powers of Aladdin's lamp are denied us.   This is true of the lowest and the highest spirits, and in this respect none are superior to man."

There are, in the testimony of seers and spirits, the imperfections and discrepancies that are natural to the human mind in all degrees and spheres of progressive life.   The fixed laws of truth, as appreciated by the philosophical reason, eventually explain and settle all doubts.   Read all sides, prove all things, and hold fast to that which is rational and good.   In this connection the affirmations of another writer* are required :—

" While every orb inhabited by human races throughout the immensities of space presents, when viewed from celestial appearance, during its first great human epoch or day, an undivided heavenly sphere, encompassing it without rent or seam, there is visible to the spiritual left of the planet earth the likeness of a divided spheroid, and beyond this two others. These are called, in heavenly language, the lower earths of spirits. Also, to spiritual appearance, are visible their opposite semicircles, *three* in number, and they are called the upper earths of spirits.   The three hemispheres of the lower spiritual earth of the planet are composed of natural, intellectual, and moral disorders; and upon

---

* See "Arcana of Christianity," by Rev. T. L. Harris, p. 150, Sec. 265, 266, *et seq.*

their surfaces all such of its inhabitants as have left the natural form, in inmost repugnance to Divine good and truth, by the voluntary acceptance of evil as their good, become confirmed in the inversion of the Divine law, and divested of such apparent vestiges of good and truth as cohere, on leaving earth, to their minds.

" The three semicircles which are opposite appear in spiritual representations as three immense, extended spaces, the one beyond the other, inhabited temporarily by such inhabitants of earth as, through willingness to become purified of all evils, are gradually putting off the remains of evils acquired in the world, and passing into the fullness of regeneration, which, when attained, qualifies them to become angels.   It must be understood that this view is an accommodation to the present condition of the human mind, and falls far short of the stupendous reality.   In this same accommodated view we behold beyond the outermost and nethermost of the spheres of the lower earth the real hells of the planet, which are extended on three planes corresponding to the inversions of the natural, spiritual, and celestial degrees in man—three infernal abodes."

The arrangement of the three heavens and the three hells, above and below the primary and ultimate regions of the earth, the writer further explains thus:

E.—Heavens of the Planet.	E
D.—Superior region of the Upper Earth of Spirits.	D
C.—Intermediate region of the Upper Earth of Spirits.	C
B.—Ultimate region of the Upper Earth of Spirits.	B
O—Natural Earth.	Earth. O
F.—Primary region of the Lower Earth of Spirits.	F
G.—Intermediate region of the Lower Earth of Spirits.	G
H.—Final region of the Lower Earth of Spirits.	H
I.—Hells of the Planet.	I

Without comment we pass on to take testimony from the record of a distinguished medium;* although, before introducing the dialogue, we are constrained to remark that the Spirit communicating seems not to

---

* Through whom Judge Edmonds received a large variety of communications.

have investigated for himself, and thus does not really know, what he gives to the inquirer. The first is a Skeptic; the second the Spirit communicating.

SKEPTIC.—If you are able to learn the abstruse things you state, I see no difficulty in your learning any thing that a spirit may know—you might gather the most sublime truths of the eternal world.

SPIRIT.—True, if I could converse with those who know those sublime truths. [Here, very candidly, the Spirit confesses a lack of knowledge.]

SKP.—And why can you not? If they can tell you one thing they can another.

SP.—Yes; just as easy as a man who is six feet high can be seven. The spirits I talk with are persons of good education, and they can tell me facts in astronomy or in any of the sciences, as easily as they could answer me the most trifling question. My spirit friends are generally those whom I knew on earth. I seek only for such things as any well-educated spirit could tell me, facts concerning spirit-life. As to the sublime truths you speak of, they are continually given to mortals in the ordinary mode of inspiration; for there is no mortal that is not occasionally inspired. The great truths are ever dawning upon us—and rarely, as I think, does a truth come to the world of spirits that is not immediately conveyed to earth by thousands who wish to inspire their cherished friends. The one great truth that spirits have to tell us is, that they are often with us and do communicate with mankind, although the recipients of their inspiration are unconscious that they are inspired. Nine out of ten of all the inventions of earth have been brought to it from a more

advanced world.   The inventors have supposed the
ideas their own, and plumed themselves accordingly,
while they were merely receiving them from their
invisible friends.

SKP.—I do not understand—according to your doctrine that spirits are like mortals, only more progressive
—how the spirits were able to make inventions, if they
could not while on earth.

SP.—Doubtless they are inspired, as we are.   They
often tell me that they speak as they are impressed or
inspired to speak.   Many of them claim to be impressible mediums, and to be able at any time to hold communication with the Lythylli.

SKP.—And what are the Lythylli?

SP.—Spirits of the next estate.   Spirits who have
terminated their career in the spirit-worlds, and gone to
a system of worlds in the next degree of sublimation—
worlds as much more refined as their bodies are when
they have become Lythylli,—as spirits call those above
them.   They are those who have departed that life,
and returned to converse with those they left behind.

SKP.—And those Lythylli doubtless talk with beings
in a condition above them.

SP.—Of course, and so on, up to God.   Many a
thought uttered on earth is freshly brought from the
highest source of inspiration.

SKP.—You will admit then that the books of the Old
Testament may have been inspired by God.

SP.—I have always claimed that they were inspired.
It was not the Creator that spoke directly to man.   The
truths and the commandments which start at the fountain of wisdom do not always arrive at earth in their

original purity.   And yet as a rule the truth comes to us as fast as we can receive it, and as pure as we can bear it.   There is not one mind in a million that is capable of receiving truth in its purity.   It requires a very high development of all the faculties to open the mind to its comprehension.

SKP.—I should like hereafter to discuss this matter further, but now I am chiefly interested in the later questions that have been before us.   I am interested in your system of *astronomy*.   If there were a possibility of demonstration or proof, how we might extend the science!   As a spirit man might visit the stars personally, instead of peeping at them through telescopes.

SP.—Yes, a few of them, but the great majority of them are as far beyond a spirit's reach as they are from ours.   Remember that a spirit, placed upon a globe which is 100,000,000,000 miles from us, looks upon a sky almost identical with ours.   The only difference is probably the substitution of the planets of the spirit-systems for those of ours.   The fixed stars are the same to them as they are to us, being entirely too distant to change their relative position.   Perhaps observations made on earth and upon a spirit-world 100,000,000,000 miles distant would by the parallax determine the distance of many of the stars.   But we well know there are millions of stars that could not be surveyed from so narrow a base.

SKP.—Cannot spirits visit the fixed stars?

SP.—Some of them are near enough to be visited; Sirius, for example.

SKP.—What is the difficulty? can they not move with the swiftness of thought?

Sp.—Doubtless they can, through a vacuum such as the stellar spaces. The difficulty is to think fast enough. A spirit of strong will and great power can move through space with great rapidity. His will-force is the motive power, and there is nothing to resist his progress. He can go in a second of time a distance quite incomprehensible to himself, and yet before he reaches the fixed stars some time will have been consumed.

Skp.—You spoke of talking with a spirit who had visited Sirius. Did he tell you any thing of it?

Sp.—Yes. It is larger than our sun by a third. It has a more extensive system of planets than we have. The people inhabiting them did not seem to him any more progressed than the people of earth, and he was not so much pleased with the races he saw as he was with our own Hellenic race. Only by visiting many worlds can we become liberalized. A spirit only can be truly cosmopolitan. This astronomer, who had with a company of others visited Sirius, learned that the machinery of that system of worlds was like ours. It had its accompanying solar system for the residence of spirits, and the successive systems for the Lythylli. It was one of the many systems that with ours wheel round a great and distant center, forming together one of the many congeries of systems that revolve in almost eternal years round a still greater center, which with all the masses of worlds created roll round the central orb of the universe.

Skp.—This is a fine picture. I can imagine myself located in space, and looking upon the worlds which like motes in the sunbeam fill the universe of God.

Sp.—If you were able to take in at a glance the

whole creation, you would certainly find its movements beautiful. Suppose the suns with their planets to form a disc. Suppose the systems of spirit-worlds many in number to lie parallel to the grosser solar systems upon which human beings originate. These discs move through space in a platoon, side by side. They do not advance in a line perpendicular to their discs, but parallel to them. All spheres having a common origin must revolve in the same general direction. The rotation upon their axes is also governed by an invisible law, for there was no chance-work in the great arrangements of the heavens. In no other way than this edgewise movement could the systems move so safely and so well.

Skp.—Tell me something of the manner in which spirits go and come between earth and the spirit-world.

Sp.—Let us premise, that when a spirit of earth sets his foot upon the globe destined for his second life he finds himself standing upon solid ground. He walks upon it as he would have walked upon earth, and he soon forgets the change of his condition. The world he walks on is as solid to him as this earth was to him when he was here. There are rocks and trees, water and earth, fruits and flowers around him as there were on earth, and he must have a good memory indeed if he do not soon cease to think of his new abode otherwise than to feel how much happier he is. He walks upon the ground, and he steps with as firm a tread as ever he did, and he weighs as much.

Skp.—How is it when he leaves earth for his home?

Sp.—It requires little effort. He rises into the atmosphere about as high as the clouds above them, when the sky is not clear, until he can see his direction. He then provides for the sustenance of his lungs, and darts off toward the sun of his system, which is always clearly visible, like a very large star, shining with a soft light easily recognized as from a spirit's sun. In a few seconds after starting that sun, expands upon his view and the planets of the system become visible. He sees the globe which is his destination, and directs his course to it. Its southern hemisphere is toward him as he approaches from earth, and as he nears it he turns to that part of it.

SKP.—You say the spirit-sun is visible from here. Where in the heavens is it situated?

SP.—It is within the constellation Ursa Major (called sometimes Dipper), near the pole-star. The two stars at the outer end of the cup are called the pointers, because they indicate the direction in which to find the pole-star: the spirit-sun is seen over the open cup of the Dipper, about one-third of the apparent distance from the line of the cup that the pointers are apart, and rather nearer to the handle end of the cup than the outer end. A line from our sun to that star would, I think, be found to be the true North. Possibly the vibratory change in the magnetic pole of our earth would be accounted for by the revolutions round the spirit-sun of the larger planets of that system. Possibly the magnetic pole of the earth would be at the axis but for the vast accumulations of the metals in the locality of the magnetic pole. If these matters were all understood, all the phenomena of earth-magnetism would be clear to us.

SKP.—There must be parts of our earth where spirits cannot so easily see their sun.

SP.—Yes, in the southern hemisphere. The earth

would then be between. He would have to go off the
semi-diameter of the earth to see it, if he started from
the South pole.

SKP.—I have understood you to say that the world
upon which spirits from earth generally reside is not so
large as this.

SP.—Yes, Juno is six thousand five hundred miles in
diameter. Its moon is two thousand miles in diameter
and one hundred and eighty thousand miles distant from
Juno. To the inhabitants of earth is apportioned the
planet Juno, to the inhabitants of our moon is apportioned the satellite of Juno, to the inhabitants of Venus
and Mercury is given Iris, the first planet from the sun.

SKP.—You spoke of the inhabitants of the moon. I
thought there was no atmosphere there, and that, therefore, no life could exist there ?

SP.—The side turned from us is inhabited. The side
turned toward us has no visible atmosphere, no water,
and no life.

SKP.—How can that be ?

SP.—The center of gravity of the moon is seven miles
out of the center of the mass. That throws one side
out fourteen miles, and making an equivalent of a
mountain of that height. Although the atmosphere in
the moon may reach thirty or forty miles, yet at the
height of fourteen miles it would be insufficient to sustain life, and it would moreover be intensely cold. The
side thus projecting is attracted toward the earth, and
thus we never see but one side. On the other side,
however, there are soil, atmosphere, water, and vegeta
ble and animal life, as on this earth.

SKP.—I feel continually a disposition to ask you how

7

you know these matters, such as the condition of the other side of the moon, which has never been seen by mortal eye, but you will reply that spirits have told you so. This I cannot realize, for my friends do not come back from heaven to instruct me. I wish, without pausing to controvert your statements, to hear all that you have to say about the astronomy of the spirit-world. You have, I suppose, learned the exact distance of heaven from earth?

Sp.—I think I have been correctly informed. I must depend on the statements made to me, and wait till the multitude of statements shall be received as proof. The distance of the spirit-world from this solar system is stated to be 103,000,000,000. The size of their sun is 1,204,088 miles. Its apparent size to an observer on earth is about the same as that of our planet Venus.

Skp.—The greatest difficulty I find in all your theory is learning to think of the invisible and intangible substance of a spirit's body as a real solid thing. It seems nearer to nonentity.

Sp.—We cannot easily comprehend a condition of matter which we have never had opportunity to examine. As we cannot see it nor feel it, it is natural to ignore its existence. Many a time in the period of your life have comets swept across the heavens. You have distinctly seen them with the naked eye. One which you saw was 50,000 miles in diameter, and of so rare a substance that a star of the sixth magnitude was seen through its center. Now as the lightest cloud will hide such a star, it proves that the density of that little fleck of cloud was more in that small space than in the 5,000 miles depth of the mass of the comet. Indeed, it is not unreasonable to suppose that a room full of gas or smoky air would, out in space, expand to the dimensions of that comet, and be visible at the distance of a hundred millions of miles. You can and do comprehend all that, because the matter in question is gross matter, though exceedingly rare. If it were sublimated matter, however dense, the light of the sun would not reflect from it, and therefore you would ignore its existence because it required the eyes of philosophy to see it. Remember that matter, though sublimated, is still matter, and is subject to all the natural laws, just as absolutely as the infinitesimal quantity of matter in the rarer comets, which forms itself into a sphere and travels through space like a solid planet. Nature does not excuse any particle of matter from obedience. If there be but one particle of matter to make a world, that particle must obey the law.

Skp.—I am inclined to believe with you that all matter in the universe, whether gross or refined, is subject to the natural laws: I can, therefore, though with difficulty, comprehend that the globes wherever reside the spirits of the departed, may be real substantial matter. I begin to see that it must be so, that spirit must have a solid world to live on, as we have, else the conditions necessary to their happiness could not be found.

Sp.—I am gratified that you have surmounted the old prejudices so common, I might almost say universal, in the world. Assuredly not one in a thousand ever thinks or reasons upon the nature of a future life. Men muse and dream about it, but the result of all is a few fantastic glittering palaces built in the clouds, so very frail and unsubstantial that they vanish like a spirit at the first breath of common sense.

CHAPTER XIV.

A PHILOSOPHICAL VIEW OF THE SUMMER LAND.

An inspired discourse on this theme comes to us with a number of cogent passages.* The speaker is moved to consider the question of elementary spirit and elementary matter, and to adduce arguments in favor of the hypothesis that the original and primordial substance was spirit. Some writers, he proceeds to say, make.a distinction between matter and spirit—between the elemental particles of the two substances. Now, one of two things is certain : If the two substances, matter and spirit, were primordial and distinct entities, then neither is infinite, but finite—limited and bounded. That is to say, the elements of matter are limited, and therefore do not pervade the universe. But they do occupy points of space. Now, it is a mathematical axiom that two substances cannot occupy the same point of space at the same time. But these writers tell us that spiritual substance, so-called, fills another portion of the universe. Now, no mind can suppose that a particle of spiritual substance, which is real, can occupy the same point of space that matter occupies. What follows? Why, that spirit itself is not infinite. Thus we have presented, not a universe, but a dual-verse of living matter on one

---

* The extracts in this chapter are from a Lecture by the inspired S. J. Finney, delivered in New York, March 27, 1864.

side and living spirit on the other. Can matter be in-spired by spirit, if the two are radically distinct and both finite? Where is our infinity? It is only two finites. Where is the divine intelligence? Where is God? Where is religion? Where is our immortality? It is a logical impossibility. The truth is this: Man is immortal only because he is the incarnation of the Divine substance, and since that is infinite, he cannot any more be dissolved than the universe can be.

On this subject of elementary matter and spirit, let me quote the words of an immortal :—*

" The spiritual body is a substance; and yet it is not what you term ' matter.' Spirit bears the same relation to earthy matter that light sustains to the element of water — the same as the form to the ground which enlivens it. The spiritual body is 'matter' spiritual-ized ; as the flower is the earth refined."

Observe the phraseology : " The spiritual body is matter spiritualized." Now I am going to analyze this statement, and see if it will stand the test of investiga-tion.

The Harmonial Philosophy does not teach us that the words of an immortal are absolute authority on theo-retical or philosophical questions. We take them like any other authority, and we put questions to spirit personages as though they were here on earth. If the spirit-body is matter (in the ordinary signification of the term) " spiritualized," then what follows ? Why, that what you call matter is spirit materialized. Action and reaction are equal and correlative in the

---

* See a volume by the Author, entitled " The Present Age and Inner Life." p. 124.

dynamics of the universe. The sun's auric waves break into zones and the zones into planets, and from the planets come satellites. Mark the recent developments of science—how they sustain the Harmonial Philosophy. Twenty years ago "Nature's Divine Revelations" announced: "In the beginning the Univercœlum was one boundless, undefinable, and unimaginable ocean of liquid fire." What are the late revelations of science? That the motions of the planets are the mechanical equivalent of the heat exhausted from the sun; that four hundred and fifty-three four hundred and fifty-fourths of this gravitating tendency has already been wasted as heat. Only one four hundred and fifty-fourth of the original heat of the whole solar system remains to us as gravity. Yet if this one four hundred and fifty-fourth were converted into heat, it would raise the temperature of a mass of water, equal to the sun and planets in weight, *twenty-eight millions of degrees centigrade*. The heat of the lime light is two thousand degrees centigrade; think of a temperature equal to *two million degrees centigrade* —if you can. The gravitation of worlds is the result of the heat lost. If our entire system were pure carbon, its combustion would generate only one three thousand five hundredths of twenty-eight million degrees centigrade. So the mechanical motion of the heavens is always the complement of the heat lost. Therefore the present state of the universe is the result of condensation.

Science is proving that the now solid worlds were once in such a fine, ethereal state, that no external senses that man possesses could have revealed their elemental existence to him. Body had not appeared. It came at last, by cooling and condensation — or by " materialization."

Conversely—take water, raise its temperature till it becomes steam: Can you see it? Out of that steam unfold electricity; out of that, magnetism; and so on, one substance after another, until you reach the limits of external science—where will you stop? Nowhere this side of the original state of what you call " matter," which state is an infinite remove from " body," and can be called by no other name but spirit [essence?].

Now, what is "matter?" I answer, It is a word which ought to be applied not to the original substratum of things, but only to the *form* or *body* of things. It is a misuse of the word to apply it to the primordial and eternal elements of the universe. It is a word derived from the action of the senses upon the *phenomena* of body only. It, therefore, relates only to body. But what is body? Gross material? No. Heat a granite rock in your retort; analyze it; what do you get? Gases. Put any thing through a chemical analysis, and what do you get? Not body, but a gaseous substance. And the more critically and thoroughly you carry your analysis, the less do you see of what you call " matter." Your granite rock is so changed that, instead of having gravitation, it ascends and escapes outward into the universe. Its specific gravity is changed into specific levity. The signification, therefore, which you attach to "matter," is unphilosophical. It is a word derived from the experience of the senses. Original elements are eternal, and cannot, therefore, be seen by the senses, for they are limited by space and time. And how can faculties limited under space and time reveal the existence of elements which know neither space nor time? Chronological functions are correlated only with chronological phenomena. *Only Pure Reason can know Pure Being; for Pure Reason alone is consciousness of Pure Being. Pure Intelligence is Pure Being knowing itself.* Sensation knows only phenomena. It is, therefore, only in pure intelligence, or spirit, that being is known. Body is the phenomenon miscalled "matter." The word "matter," therefore, derived, as it is, only from the action of the senses, means only phenomena. Pure intelligence is, therefore, the only primordial stuff of things—the one eternal substance at the basis of all bodies. And this I call pure spirit. And by inductive science this pure spirit can never be reached, for it is an infinite distance (in time) removed from the phenomena of mere body. Eternity alone could suffice to complete the empiricle process backward and inward to this great center of the Cosmos. But man is pure spirit in his inmost, and hence pure being is revealed directly, at once, in consciousness itself.

But let us go a step further. Science is proving by induction that these external material forms are only appearances of fine, ethereal, everlasting essences. The "material" world is only spirit materialized, condensed, and made up into forms under light and shadow. It is nothing but the image of the infinite perfection. It is not spirit that you *see* and *touch* with your fingers; it is the body, the shadow, the form. I grant you it is real to your senses, but real what?

Answer: Real phenomena. Hence you see the view I take that the only substance in the universe, in the first instance, must be Spirit. Whatever it may become afterwards, in appearance, in phenomenon, in manifestation, whether it be in the solar atmosphere breaking off into waves and circles of suns, one after the other, from the great vortex of the Univercœlum, or the systems of planetary worlds derived from the great central source, or the vegetation and the animal life that exists on those planets, it is all one original stuff emanating from the great Central Sun, through ever-expanding circles toward the circumference. But action and reaction are equal, and if these material worlds are spirit materialized, then the spirit-spheres are body spiritualized. We cannot have a spiritualizing or upward process until we have a materializing or downward process. These are complements of each other. One is attained by the translation of heat into the mechanical motions of the heavens, while the attainment of spiritual development, or the spirit-spheres, is but regaining the heat so lost. And you will find, as you rise through the sphere of immortal life, that you are departing from mere mechanics — that, as you approach nearer and nearer the impersonal God—the Divine Intelligence—you flee farther and farther from the limited and bounded ; that the shadows of these material bodies are disappearing, while the reascending energies of this one only substance are unfolding spirit.

The Spirit-world is developed by a reverse complementary action of the "materializing" process. The spiritualizing process must repeat on a higher scale, in reverse order, the cycles of the career of world build-

7*

ing, because action and reaction are equal. These worlds come out of the solar atmosphere, being condensed from vast solar rings. Science confirms this view; every step of its progress brings us more and more near to this great general truth. Now what follows? That the spirit-sphere which emanates from this grosser "material" sphere, and constitutes the second sphere, or Summer Land, must be created by a process exactly the reverse of that by which the earth and other planets are produced.

Science teaches us that the whole solar system was once filled with solar ether, and was itself a portion of a vast zone of some far-off stellar center, and that the process of world-formation was by the breaking up of these zones of solar atmosphere into planetary bodies. What, then, must be the spiritual process, but a re-smelting, a disintegration of the elements, and a rolling of them back, through successive stages, toward the great Central Sun of the universe again, but in a higher plane? You must have a process of building the spirit-sphere exactly the reverse of that of building these planetary worlds. And when you realize this law of analogy, you will see how *vast* must be that second sphere—the Summer Land.

Now, in regard to this subject, I consider that some minds have fallen into a most illogical mistake in locating the Summer Land. Although one writer admits fully the principle that spirit emanations from the earth ascend and form another sphere, yet he locates the spirit-zone immediately around the earth's equator, and makes it only sixty degrees wide. Now two millions of human beings pass to the Spirit-world from this

earth every year, making for every century two hundred millions. Geology is teaching us that man has
inhabited this planet at least one hundred thousand
years. Stretch your eyes down the future for one hundred thousand more. Consider two hundred thousand
years as the probable life of the world. Then consider
the increase of population for one hundred thousand
years to come, and say if you can that such a sphere is
adequate for the teeming millions of this earth. Can
you find sufficient space for that number of beings in a
zone sixty degrees wide around the equator, at the distance of the moon? Such a limited spirit-sphere finds
no response in reason.

There is another objection to this limited view of the
Summer Land. It makes the highest sphere of the
Spirit-world reach just beyond the moon. Now,
though the moon is not yet inhabited, the time may
come when it will be, and a spirit-sphere evolved from
that satellite. What will be the consequence? The
two spheres of the earth and the moon will run into one
another, creating utter confusion in spiritual geography.

But this conception of the dimensions of the Summer Land is far too contracted. Look out upon this
boundless universe of God. How many peopled worlds
are swinging through the vast ocean of immensity!
Shall there be no unitive World where all these peoples
associate? Are we to be confined to this little speck
of earth, this mote of shadow in the everlasting sunbeam? Why has God given me my social nature, if I
am not to feel the waves of affection that float from the
immortal Societies arisen from *other* worlds? And what
room have I for immortal associations on such a little

spiritual sphere as that which is supposed to environ this planet? No, no; give me a sphere vast enough to infold all the relations of the innumerable worlds of the universe—a space commensurate with the grandeur and glory and vastness of that universe—a universal Summer Land.

But further, against this limited notion, the Spirit-world is made up of the aggregate emanations, in zonal forms, of all the teeming planets of one great circle of suns, each one of which contributes its quota of spirit-ualized elements. As you approach a flower-garden, you first discover it by your senses. You cannot see the emanations of its life. I have seen the flaming aura of these forms in Nature. A handful even of dead earth has its emanations, because it is undergoing a process of change and translation. So with all the forms of earth; the elements rise, and they can never entirely come back again. Some of the grosser constituents may settle near the earth, and become reorganized, but the entire elements never return. The earth, as it revolves through space, become more dense; its inner life is flowing from it; where does it go? Out into space, like an aura. The currents of these material elements flow first toward the north, where, by process of refinement, getting eliminated, they rise into the higher atmosphere and flow southward. You may see these emanations, by means of spirit-vision, sweeping toward the south pole, surging toward the spiritual zone, moving upward into the vast magnificent ocean of the spirit-sphere, and thus forming a vast zonal circle called the Summer Land. It is a step toward the Divine Center, a translation from the condition of cold, gross matter. It is a process of eliminating what you call "matter" into spirit, unfolding its powers and qualities, and making it real, substantial, perfect, and beautiful. Hence the relation between the Spirit-world and this earth, or other earths, that are peopled or unpeopled, must be first an elemental relation. We talk about the vastness and magnificence of our Mississippi River. Do you suppose there are no rivers of finer and more ethereal waters in the Spirit-world? Years ago angels told me: "Could you open your spirit-eyes, you would see vast rivers of magnetic or spiritual life rolling from the planets toward the spirit-home in the universe—flowing from these solid worlds to make up the elements of the spheres." On the bosoms of these rivers the elementary particles of refined organisms ascend. But man alone as a personality ascends. Why? Because he alone is a microcosm. The other forms contribute elements; man contributes his personality. This world is joined to the other by positive and negative laws, just as the magnetic current between the two poles of a battery connects the two ends, and each is indispensable to the other in the grand process of change and of cosmical spirit-elevation.

CHAPTER XV.

THE SPIRITUAL ZONES AMONG THE STARS.

A CLAIRVOYANT looking into space from the earth sees a great number of shining belts in different directions. These nebulous rings in the sky, which diminish and increase, symmetrically, as they recede from and approach to their respective aphelions and perihelions, mislead clairvoyants, mediums, and even many spirits, with respect to the location and dimensions of the different spirit-worlds. The cause of conflicting testimony is thus disclosed. The first year or more of my own observations I was frequently mistaken on these identical points. The judgment improves in the state of clairvoyance the same as under any other educational stimulation.

Almost every star or globe, like the earth, has one or more meteoric belts revolving around the planet's body, and in appearance similar to the rings of Saturn. They are variable in magnitude, in brightness, and apparently in the order or periodicity of their revolution. (In a future volume these grand heavenly wonders will be treated at length.) The general principle is, that the planets double their distances as they recede from the sun. Between the orbits of Earth and Mars there is a space of about 50,000,000 miles in width, and between Mars and Jupiter's orbit there is an interval of "airy nothing" not less than 319,000,000 of miles broad. In this space we observe a vast bright belt of apparently continuous solid matter, which, upon closer examination, is revealed as *a river of small stars* flowing, or revolving like numerous other rings, around the positive sun of our system. This splendid panorama of stellar beauties I formerly supposed might be the " Second Sphere." But further growth in clairvoyance sharpened the discriminating faculties, and thus the circle of asteroids in that portion of the heavens became clearly understood.   There are about 31,400,000 miles of space between the orbits of Venus and Mercury.   In this interval, also, as between Mercury and the Sun, I perceive *rivers of cometary bodies*—looking like the gorgeous rings of Saturn, only far more loaded with the red flames of fire, and a kind of blazing ether, from which a vast white reflection is sometimes spread through the whole southern hemisphere of the heavens. Some seers have supposed (and myself among them) that one of these broad continuous asteroidal rings was the real spirit-world belonging to our earth.   More accurate information, however, conveys new ideas of magnitudes and relations ; and the first Summer Land is found to be revolving near the grand orbit of the Milky Way.

There is something to be learned from the law of gravitation—the weight and the lightness of bodies— by which law the logical and mathematical reason can approximately locate the Solid Spiritual Zone in space. The philosophy of the schools [see Comstock and other authors] teaches that the force of gravity is greatest at the surface of the earth, and decreases both upward and downward but in different degrees.   It decreases above the surface as the square of the distance from the center increases. From the surface to the center it decreases, simply as the distance increases. That is, gravity at the surface of the earth (which is about 4,000 miles from the center) is four times more powerful than it would be at double that distance, or 8,000 miles from the center. According to the principles just stated, a body which at the surface of the earth weighs a pound, at the center of the earth will weigh nothing.

1,000 miles from the center it will weigh $\frac{1}{4}$ of a pound,
2,000   "   "   "   "   "   " $\frac{1}{2}$ of a pound,
3,000   "   "   "   "   "   " $\frac{3}{4}$ of a pound,
4,000   "   "   "   "   "   "   1 pound,
8,000   "   "   "   "   "   " $\frac{1}{2}$,
12,000   "   "   "   "   "   " $\frac{1}{3}$, and so on.

The force of gravity is absolutely greatest at the center of the earth; but at that point it is exerted in all directions, and consequently a body at that point would remain stationary, because there is no superior attraction for it to obey.

Conversely, ascending into the atmosphere, the higher the rarer, and yet, as " the force of gravity is absolutely greatest at the center," so at the highest point of our atmosphere a *new density* exists from which, as a basis, a new action of the law is developed. Popular science presented the atmospheric scale thus :—

Altitude in Miles.							Density.
0	.	.	.	.	.	.	1
7	.	.	.	.	.	.	$\frac{1}{4}$
14	.	.	.	.	.	.	$\frac{1}{16}$
21	.	.	.	.	.	.	$\frac{1}{64}$
28	.	.	.	.	.	.	$\frac{1}{256}$
35	.	.	.	.	.	.	$\frac{1}{1024}$
70	.	.	.	.	.	.	$\frac{1}{1000000}$
105	.	.	.	.	.	.	$\frac{1}{1000000000}$
140	.	.	.	.	.	.	$\frac{1}{1000000000000}$
etc.							etc.

From this table it will be seen, says Prof. Kirkwood, that at the height of 35 miles the air is one thousand times rarer than at the surface of the earth; and that, supposing the same rate of decrease to continue, at the height of 140 miles the rarity would be one trillion times greater. The atmosphere, however, is not unlimited. When it becomes so rare that the force of repulsion between its particles is counterbalanced by the earth's attraction, no further expansion is possible. To determine the altitude of its superior surface is a problem at once difficult and interesting.

Science has recognized the probability of what to the clairvoyants has been long well known, that the interplanetary spaces are filled with a refined and elastic ether, through which all planets revolve, and by which a perfectly electrical and magnetic sympathy is established between all inhabited planets and the Summer Land.

The plane of the orbit of the Summer Land appears to be at an angle of 20° with that of the sun. [The volume on "Astronomy," which I hope to reach some time not far future, will contain these facts more in detail.] The sidewise appearance of the Spiritual Zone, and also its appearance as a stratified belt, are indicated in the illustrations already presented. The remarks of Humboldt, in his *Cosmos*, vol. 1, p. 126, concerning the solar light are here in order: Those who have lived for many years in the zone of palms, must retain a pleasant impression of the mild radiance with which the Zodiacal Light, shooting pyramidally upward, illumines a part of the uniform length of tropical nights. I have seen it shine with an intensity of light equal to the

Milky Way in Sagittarius, and that not only in the rare and dry atmosphere of the summits of the Andes, at an elevation of from thirteen to fifteen thousand feet, but even on the boundless grassy plains, the Llanso of Venezuela, and on the sea-shore, beneath the ever clear sky of Cumana.

In another place this author brings out something equally important: " Great as is the obscurity which still envelops the material cause of the Zodiacal Light, still, however, with the mathematical certainty that the solar atmosphere cannot reach beyond nine-twentieths of the distance of Mercury—the opinion supported by Laplace, Schubert, Arago, Poisson, and Biot, according to which the Zodiacal Light radiates from a vapory flattened ring, freely revolving in space between the orbits of Venus and Mars, appears, in the very deficient state of observation, to be the most satisfactory . . . No telescope has yet indicated any sidereal character in the vaporous, rotating, and flattened ring of the Zodiacal Light. Whether the particles of which this ring consists, and which, according to some, are conceived to rotate upon themselves, in obedience to dynamic conditions, and, according to others, merely to revolve around the sun, are illumined or self-luminous, like many kinds of terrestrial vapors, is a question as yet undecided."

Leaving upon the reader's mind these few suggestive words from a scientific authority, I pass on to consider other branches of this beautiful tree of stellar truth.

CHAPTER XVI.

TRAVELING AND SOCIETY IN THE SUMMER LAND.

THE human Will, having by constitution and relation a "power" which is higher than organic "force," can overcome the force of material gravity, and attain a buoyancy in accordance with the refinements and tides of the ethereal rivers of space, and thus the individual may rise bodily, and float like a person bathing and floating in a beautiful stream in summer-time. The spirit-body, remember, floats on the bosom of these flowing celestial streams. Upon the celestial current the spirit moves with the speed of light. Individuals so borne along testify that they experience or realize *no motion*, unless they approach and glide past an orb or other body in space. One celestial traveler said that he was conscious of moving or floating at the rate of what seemed to be not more than a mile an hour; another said that she was not conscious of any motion at all; and yet it was asserted that both were "flying through space millions of miles an hour, three times farther than from here to the sun, inside of one hundred and twenty-five minutes!" A voyage on the celestial seas may be accomplished quicker than a telegraph-operator could record the fact for the daily press.

Birds, you know, ride beautifully through the atmosphere; sometimes without so much as moving their wings. Certain winged ones can keep themselves moving through the air by means of the momentum accumulated by the previous use of their strong electrical wings. You observe that these peculiar birds work their wings vigorously and rapidly before they suspend their motions, and commit themselves wi:h such beautiful confidence to the buoyancy and integrity of the viewless air. This fact in outward creation illustrates the principle of traveling by spirit will-power. Birds of loftiest flight work upon and frictionize the air on the same principle as the glass cylinder in "a magnetic machine" works against the silken cushions. According to my investigation, birds develop themselves into Leyden-jars. All birds, by the motions of their wings in the act of flying, fill their bodies and very bones with essential electricity. Their feathers are non-conductors, and thus the electricity or essence which they collect is not easily exhausted. Birds cannot easily bring their forces and wills to bear against a strong current of air, but they accomplish the whole feat of aërial navigation sufficiently to illustrate the principle of post-mortem traveling on these celestial currents. Birds of flight bring the electrical principle of the atmosphere into the finest tissues and air-chambers of their hollow bones. Ornithologists find that the bones of birds are supplied with nothing substantial to the eye. Some suppose they are filled with air ; yes, just as a Leyden-jar is filled with electricity. Through the spreading and vibrations of their wings they develop electricity and discharge it, as the electric eel discharges the subtile current without communicating any shock to itself. These birds, unless they have untrammeled opportunities to expand and vibrate their wings, and thus to ascend and fly, have no buoyancy. Like heavy domestic fowls, if you clip one of their wings, or in any way accustom them to the foot-exercises of a yard-life, they seem to lose the power of working up the magnetic forces, whereby they gather the more external electric or buoyant principle. Domestic birds do not lose this power, but they lose the habit of flying, and therefore have no more buoyancy than any wingless bodies of similar weight. It is possible for earth's present inhabitants to realize what I am now stating—the ability, not bodily to fly through the air exactly as birds do by means of wings, but in harmony with the buoyant electric principle, and by a wise employment of this sovereign "power" which is implanted in spirit, with which all may measurably conquer circumstances. By this "power," mankind, preserving each his own peculiar life and individuality, in harmony with those invariable celestial river-tides, or currents, will be enabled after death to travel from the Summer Land to different departments of the heavens so filled with orbs, and to visit what would seem to be immeasurable localities and interminable avenues with more ease, naturalness, and infinitely more pleasure, than you can now travel from your home to foreign places on this globe.

Again, this power of the spirit's will is marvelous in a chemical point of view. Do you suppose that the good Father has made mankind to live no more than "three-score and ten years," and that then the whole life and temple of each one will be utterly destroyed? No! man is built to live an hundred years. But the finest piece of mechanism possible to conceive is this spiritual constitution of man. Will it cease to be of service? It has been urged many times that this world is but the rudimental existence. Do you not see that these crude and unsatisfactory adaptations—these undisciplined and ungoverned elements of character—are only in their elementary state? Mankind require germination and development from the inmost. The love of art, like art itself in this world, is but prophetic. If a man's spirit yearns to paint the Madonna so that she would seem to others' eyes to be a loving, breathing, palpitating lady of heaven, and yet but a work of art on insensate canvas, is this yearning not a prophecy to his own love-laden soul that the intense aspirations which the good Father implanted shall find ultimate gratification? In a word, is it not plainly saying to the spirit that, by means of that "power" which shall be unfolded from within, he will develop as perfect a "form" as he had conceived as possible on the canvas, and, indeed, infinitely more holy, loving, breathing, adorable, and heavenly?

Spiritual investigators in America have had a great many demonstrations of this form-making power of spirit within the last ten years. The illustrations have been furnished by many spirits of great intelligence, of power over the chemical affinities of the air. Persons who have taken no interest in either Science or Art, will *not* be able soon "after death" to do these almost magical or miraculous things with imponderable principles. It is said that a great many inhabitants in the Summer Land know nothing about what wondrous changes can be accomplished in the air by the will. I have a good mother who, although she has been there a full score of years, does not yet form a clear concep-

tion of how—that is, on what principle in matter and
mind—these "manifestations" occur, some of which
she herself has occasionally made by the senses of persons still on earth. She, an affectionate and reverential
spirit, does not apply her mind to study the *method*.
For her it is enough to know that *it can be done*, and
that, like breathing, it is productive of happiness. Is
not this natural to some minds? How many think,
when on a steamboat, of the prodigious force of the
concealed engine? Much less do persons think of the
days and years of agony and poverty and discourage-
ments which the successive inventors of that hidden
steam-machine experienced before they brought it to its
present degree of perfection. Men do not often think
of these things—of method; they only look at *ultimates*
and *results*.

So with myriads who now reside in the Summer
Land. They take particular interest in what is possible, and only see *results* that are wrought in terrestrial
circles.

In the city of New York, on many different occasions,
most beautiful transient *flowers* were chemically and
artistically formed out of suitable elements, the magnetic essences, which ever pervade the atmosphere.
These astonishing specimens of spirit workmanship were
presented to members of the circle. Each flower thus
formed was perfectly *palpable* to the bodily senses.
The different colors and odors were distinct. And the
stems and leaves could be *felt* and held in the hand.
On one occasion a spirit-flower was placed on the man-
tel, according to directions, and the member who did
it went back to the table; then the eyes of each inves-

tigator were fixed upon the flower, and in the course of twelve minutes the whole plant totally vanished!

Those who have deeply investigated are familiar with this " power of will of spirit," which can be effectually used by the wise, intelligent, and artistic. The most gifted spirits have the "power," chemically, to bring together magnetically essential particles that are floating in the human atmosphere. Thus they construct and inspire with transient animation some of the most perfect forms of beauty. And yet the mere bodily *presence* of peculiar temperaments in a circle, will utterly prevent such a manifestation. Some persons breathe in and use up the requisite particles in the atmosphere. In most instances a certain combination of imponderable principles is indispensable to such manifestations. That combination is, for the most part, accidental or fortuitous ; because even spirits, as a general thing, are not regulated by an intellectual appreciation of scientific combinations. Neither spirits from the Summer Land nor terrestrial investigators have ascertained how many of certain vital and mental temperaments should be associated to constitute a perfectly successful circle for the manifestation of palpable "forms." At present, therefore, throughout the country, the manifestation takes the form of " social intercourse." Being social, it is regulated by no intellectual by-laws, or " scientific formulas," and disorder, confusion, and contradictions are the not unfrequent consequences. But this phase of haphazard, disorderly intercourse is passing, and Spiritualists are adopting methods that will lead to a more thorough understanding of their high and glorious opportunities.

Principles are both omnipresent and impersonal. All the principles of the male and female Divinity are, therefore, impersonally present in that very spot which you now occupy. For instance, you may find where you now are all possible chemical principles—the electricities, the atmospheres, the gases, the ethers, the polarities—including the principles of vegetation—and all the forces and particles of organic life. What is the proof? The proof is, you can *breathe!* Breathing is a chemical transaction. Chemistry is at the basis of all respiration. You discharge the carbonic acid, the watery vapor, and the nitrogen, while you take in and appropriate the oxygen, which is brimming with electricity and magnetism, whereby you realize the fire and the force of the vital and cerebral systems. There, too, is a principle of vegetation. What is the proof? The proof is, that if you were to bring suitable conditions together, the process of vegetation would immediately commence. I know a German chemist, who in five days vivified a seed, that would not otherwise sprout in less than six weeks by the ordinary course of nature. He vivified it by directing upon and through it an electro-magnetic current.

The vegetative principle is beautifully illustrated by frostings on the window-glass on cold wintry nights. Reduce sufficiently the temperature of any room with window-glass exposed to the air, and forthwith the principle of vegetation will manifest itself. Next morning you find beautiful pencilings of plants, vines, and twigs with branches. The vegetable principle gathers about itself the particles which assume the forms and shapes which the principle inspires.

8

In like manner the principle of organic life is all through this world, and in every possible nook and corner of it. Take a tumbler, put in it a little wheat or rye flour, and then some water; let it stand one week in a warm atmosphere—would there not be evidences of organic life? How could it happen? Would some personal God send down the formative fiat and fix up that little flour and water so that it would begin to squirm with life? Thinkers know better. Through all parts and particles of the immeasurable universe this principle of organic life exists; only waiting conditions, forces, and suitable opportunity for a full and complete manifestation.

In this world men see the omnipresence and imper-sonality of principles crudely illustrated. But when we advance beyond this world—when we become masters of "circumstances," what may not be possible? When we rise up into perfect proprietorship; when our richest jewel will be self-possession; when we shall have the full enjoyment and complete knowledge of those attri-butes which oftentimes cause their possessor more unhappiness than gratification—when this time comes, what may we not expect?

Benjamin Franklin, the philosopher and philanthro-pist, has been recently seen in the City of New York. You would have pledged your solemn oath that he was present! And yet he may have been a million leagues from the place of "chemical manifestation." To spirit-power there is scarcely any limit. It would be difficult for any spirit to "prove an *alibi*." This is an impor-' tant point for all investigators to remember. The power of the spirit is the power for all to study. The force of the soul is not so important. The soul is organically wedged up in the body. No man's "soul" ever goes out of his body but once; then it never returns, for from that moment the body is dead. The supposition that spirits come down the shining highway and enter personally the bodies of mediums, as though mediums were automatons, is unphilosophical. Many very sensible persons have affirmed that they have "vacated" their own proper physical organizations, in order to give room for certain spirits who wished to enter. There never was a more complete misapprehension. Mediums have been permitted to say and do a great many things, because of the assumption being credited that they were not personally present in their own bodies. A multitude of Spiritualists and mediums are now recovering from the effects of such mischievous superstitions.

And yet the power of the will of a dweller of the Summer Land to make himself seen and felt at an immense distance, as though he were present in the organs of the medium's person, is almost inconceivable. It is marvelous to the unphilosophical observer. It would seem that the communicating mind was bodily and directly within the circle of your presence. The psychological connection between the medium-brain and the spirit's will is perfect. The characteristics and habits of the spirit may be transmitted to the medium —that is, when the psychological control of the brain-organs and thought-faculties of the medium is complete. The medium, for the time being, is no self-responsible individual; for the will of the communicating spirit gives *form, shape, gesture, expression,* and *speech*—all which, to an unprepared observer, looking at the matter sensuously, seems as though the controlling spirit was there embodied, and that the customary proprietor of the "organism" had departed for a time to some other place. These possessional "appearances," in this sense, are not deceptive.

Take, for example, the case of Miss ——, who has surprised, delighted, and instructed the people so often —floating them off in her golden chariots of eloquence throughout the infinitude of beautiful thoughts—how fertile her inspired brain with appropriate illustrations, and beautiful imagery, and, sometimes, with the material of profound discourse! She is an instance of what we call "inspiration"—an elevation of mentality to a place in the sphere of thought where she, personally, almost ceases to be, and where her higher impersonal faculties gather themselves to the work, just as your poetic talents and reasoning powers would act were they promoted to a higher state of freedom, impressibility, and action. Lifted out of the immediate consciousness of personality, *out of egotism*, the brain-organs and impressible thought-faculties become at once conscious of and familiar with the subject presented to them. In this state high mountains become "*a feeling.*" It is the closest identification of consciousness with principle. But mere "intellectual displays" are slowly giving way to a superior form of inspiration. The psychological power of spirit over the faculties is a question exceedingly important to all investigators. We must have a scientific basis for these spiritual temples. Purely philosophical principles can alone make these manifestations reasonable to all humanity.

The wondrous power of spirit to impress its thought at a long distance is just as natural as is conversation. Here, we do not always truly impress our thoughts. There, if the affections of two persons are in sympathy with each other, the converse is perfect. Those celestial Brotherhoods—the immense communities which I have elsewhere described—can impress each other's thoughts through immeasurable distances. But nothing of this can occur where there is no affiliation. Why not? Because of the law of attraction and repulsion. If the attraction between distant Brotherhoods is not perfect, they can form no mind-telegraphic communication with each other.

The Summer Land, more especially those portions of it which are in connection with the inhabitants of earth, appears to my interior eyes like a neighboring planet. It is the next room in the house not made with hands. But there are an infinite number of other rooms. Characteristics and peculiarities of the lower territories or sections may not prevail in any of the higher divisions of the sphere. When the eyes of the seer look higher, forthwith many of those things which so distinctly prevailed, as peculiarly adapted to the neighboring existence, utterly cease to exist, both out of the people and the scenery, as mankind progressively rise out of peculiar and special attachments, attractions, gravitations, and relations. In that section of the other sphere which lies next to us, the law of *social attraction* is as powerfully operative as it is in this world. It is not easy to tell why, but the dwellers are gregarious. They are attracted socially to remain very near each other. But higher up, or, rather, away in more refined sections, the people are influenced by other interests. In fact, the Indian-like gregariousness becomes distasteful to those who seek and encourage the finer attractions of the Summer Land. Their new and higher and larger affections render their former selfish relations almost antipathies.

The next sphere of human existence is only another department in the great educational system of eternity. There mankind have opportunities to outgrow the errors and follies of this life, and thus innumerable myriads become prepared for another ascension.* If a man leaves this world in good spiritual circumstances, he may possibly ascend at once to a better brotherhood, and be straightway engaged in higher duties, in obedience to higher sympathies and attractions. Those who can see what is "beautiful" are prepared to receive and enjoy what otherwise they could not. While those who go in darkness of spirit, who have brought upon themselves discord and misery, go there without these finer attractions and advantages, and of course they become subjects for the philanthropic treatment and attention of others who have souls for higher sympathies and the essence of a more beautiful happiness.

Individual attractions and repulsions prevail very decidedly in some sections of the upper world. They cannot be wholly conquered by will, though they may be governed. Affinities and antipathies come from the action of the temperaments of different spirits in the vicinity of each other. When you pray, therefore, be -

* In confirmation of this the reader is referred to "Death and the After Life."—last chapter, concerning the Isle of Akropanamede.

sure to pray for the _highest_ manifestation of the kingdom of heaven ; that is, for a social and national condition above the plane of these ungovernable attractions
and repulsions—for blessings above the sphere of antipathies and unwise sympathies.

The wisest lovers there make great progress by refining and elevating the persons who are the objects of
their love. But earthly minds too often _depress_ the
objects of their attraction. Is your undisguised attraction a manifestation of your love, or of your passion?
The source of your interest is perceived and realized by
the object. Suppose your attraction is not reciprocated? Why are you so forsaken, or not accepted? Because
you do not make a distinction between your love and
your passion for the object of interest. Thus many are
disappointed in the very place where they had supposed
marriage would be beautiful and friendship permanent.

There is in all this system of affection and disaffection
a fine spiritual chemistry and a subtile law of magnetism. Mankind have not yet learned the difference between mere passional inclination and true spiritual
love, which attracts and ennobles its object. The
former—the attractions of passion—are all of the
" earth, earthy." They are not found in any of the
celestial brotherhoods. The wisest do not encourage in-
discriminate inclination ; they are swayed by neither external attractions nor disinclinations. They rise up into
the celestial atmosphere of pure immortal affection.
It rules all their thoughts, and thus the wisest person in
the Summer Land is the most loving. Thus you find
that very distinguished persons, both men and women,
when they return to visit your habitations, use great

simplicity of expression. They talk mostly about love and sympathy among mankind. They seek earnestly to encourage people to cultivate greater fraternity and unity of spirit. They bestow fine and beautiful influences. But those wise ones do not often discourse on the great moral themes and momentous political questions which wholly interested them and their friends before they left the earth.

Divinity, in its central life, is LOVE. In this truth you behold the source of " salvation " to yourself and to all your neighbors in the wide world. The moment you *passionately* love your object, with a selfish and jealous desire to *exclude* all other hearts from contact with it, that moment your exclusive love becomes a chemical earthly poison. Under that changeful influence, and governed by nothing more wise than vital forces and their fiery impulses, you will surely be affected with diseases and mental distortions which may disturb your rest beyond the grave.

Mankind everywhere should *work* to bring the "kingdom of heaven on the earth"—and not *pray* for it merely. People associate together and the minister will pray. "Thy will be done on earth"—that is, "may the divine laws, and celestial principles, and heavenly methods, be carried out in human society as they are in the Summer Land." What does such a prayer amount to? Nothing, unless you put your affections and your will to *the work* of overcoming ignorance and obtaining " power " by which you can practice some portion of that which you are constantly supplicating heaven to help you to accomplish.

Fraternal love is at the bottom of true heavenly

society. Let us, then, cease being swayed by these lower attractions which constantly produce family feuds and cause a few persons to associate to the exclusion of the rest of mankind. Selfish and jealous attractions do not prevail in the best societies of the upper world. They cherish, encourage, and manifest pure love. The front pews in the heavenly society are not set apart for the rich people and the back pews for the poor ; neither do they make great distinctions in accordance with the dictates of a foolish and arbitrary fashion. They who have been servants are not treated as inferior members of the human family. While on earth, and among so-called Christians, they are treated as though they were allied closely to brutes, and not human beings; in consequence of which they are angered, and become thieves and liars, and do not hesitate to cheat and steal whenever they can.

Nothing but a radical development in society, in politics, and in religion, can ever induce some people to think deeply, and arrive at the conception that every human spirit is capable of being *pure in its love for the neighbor.* I do not mean that you can love all persons with the same kind and degree of love. I do not mean that you will ever exist without the feeling of inclination and disinclination. That would be impossible. But you need not be so warped and swayed by them as to be *poisoned* in your thoughts and affections toward those of a different nation and temperament. The true and noble in the Summer Land work diligently among the members of its inferior societies to bring about that state of heavenly peace and concord. When the inferior societies of the other sphere are har-

8*

monized, the earth-land will also be more harmonized; then all the races and peoples will begin to *feel* more of that "prayer" which is now but a lip-service among the conductors of the Churches.

The time is approaching when *mind will be supreme!* Spirit, with the power of its will and the healing of its love, is to take the ascendant. Then circumstances will be to man like the sheaves which Joseph saw in his dream, all bowing to the central sheaf; they will all bow to the master, not to the machinations of his will, not to his high animal ambitions, but only to the fine power of his spirit. When a man grows above desiring selfish ends—when he arrives at that heavenly point—then will all high and eternal things be his. And he will also own the whole world. He owns the city and the country; the sky, the ocean, and all the earth. He also becomes the proprietor of all mankind. For we are all possessors of each other in the heavenly or harmonial state.

Spiritualists have strength and inspiration adequate to the living of an entirely new life with reference to each other not only, but also with reference to all those who are not so blest—the "neighbors" who swarm in the towns, villages, cities, and different countries of the globe. They are morally and intellectually able to rise above all condemnation and misrepresentation, and be *sweet*, and *pure*, and *generous*, and *forgiving*, under all circumstances. They have but to rise up into this "feeling" that *power* in the spirit is a portion of God; that the inmost spirit only partakes of such power; that *force* is only animal; and that when you raise your hand in anger to strike another, you place

yourself on a *level* with your misdirected opponent.
For the time being you are no better than he, however
much he may be the provoker of your anger and you
the innocent party. Rise out of that combative condition. See if you cannot be strong enough to "love
your enemies" in the fine Platonic sense, which is the
most beautiful manifestation of spirit. Mankind can
never have *fraternal* festive occasions in this world
unless they attain to higher growth. The festive
seasons in the higher Societies of the Summer Land—
from 1851—to 1855 were memorable to all who witnessed
them or took part in their celestial joys. The old
Greeks, Goths, Romans, Germans, and others, forgot
the heart-hatreds that existed during the feudal period
of knight-errantry and chivalry. Many of these celestial Brotherhoods are composed of men who fell in those
desperate struggles in old England—Normans, Saxons,
Scots, Picts, Romans, Celts, French—and among them
are many of the old "Scottish Chiefs," who waged
such persistent wars in the early days of European civ-
ilization. These festive periods are perfect illustrations
of the Pentecostal times recorded by the writers of the
New Testament. Now I realize that correspondingly
joyful festive occasions are possible in this discordant
world of ours. It is an occasion when hundreds of
thousands may receive baptisms from the inhabitants
of superior spheres.

One of these celestial gatherings was in session in
1851. The first sound in my ear was music. The
melody thereof filled the whole heavens. It seemed
to fill the earth with heavenly harmony, and I became
a part of the scene. The landscapes all around me

seemed to throb and pulsate, and each part responded to every beat of the universal music. And it seemed that there were in the other world all kinds of musical instruments. The effect from the heavenly instrumentation was indescribable. But subsequently, in 1855, by most careful examination and interrogations, I found that no such thing as a musical *instrument* was ever known to exist in that part of the Summer Land. But the investigation disclosed the fact that the human voice is *a totality of sounds!* The inhabitants there have such perfect acquaintance with the powers and sounds of the voice, that, by combining the voices of particular persons, they can imitate all possible varieties and shades of instrumental music. They accomplish more than has ever entered into the heart of man to conceive. The association of harmonious voices, which is but crudely developed in this world, is one of the celestial realities.

These heavenly festive occasions seem to continue for several of our years. To them, however, it is but a short period; to us it would seem to be very long. It is a glorious Sabbath-time to them.

With them there is no account of time. An event is one beat in the universal anthem of eternal harmony. They terminate their festivals by dividing themselves up into sub-societies for the accomplishment of certain missions. Some of them accept missions to other Brotherhoods, not yet harmonized, in other and more distant parts. Others visit those who are constantly arriving from the earth, and from the planets in space. Think of the soldiers that were constantly ascending from the Union and Confederate Hospitals, and from the battle-fields, during the hours of warfare, and think, too, of the dying that is every moment going on in earthly cities—the old and infirm, the poor and the outcast, the starving and despairing—for all these the heavenly Societies are formed, and they go about their philanthropic missions. It may seem strange to some of you that any work of this kind should engage and absorb the heart-interests of the inhabitants of the Summer Land. But are not the attractions of the best faculties of human nature immortal ! | Is it not natural that good spirits, good men and good women, should divide into Societies and form themselves into Associations for the furtherance of good missions ? | Every member of the Excursional Groups has this power of Will (which I have already described), by which it is possible to travel with great speed through space. In this way some of the guardians rescue unhappy men and women who are about to shoot, or poison, or otherwise destroy themselves. A guardian angel may save some sad, lone one, who is about to drown herself in the stream. Many suicidal characters are thus saved. Many are not, however, because they cannot be approached. But there is no instance (one of them said) throughout the intricate parts of human society, where any thing of this kind occurs, but some friendly and sympathizing spirits are present, either to prevent the misfortune, or else to soothe the sad one's darkened passage on to another sphere.

So, therefore, when we each arrive in the Summer Land, we shall find persons who are perfectly acquainted with all that we have ever done ; no matter how multitudinous the floors, how thick the walls, or how

many doors were locked between us and the world—
just the same to angel-eyes as though there were no
walls, no floors, no doors, no locks—just as though all
dwelling-houses were transparent crystal palaces, instead of these thick boards and hard stones. Angels'
eyes are clairvoyant, and they can see as clearly through
the substances of space as you can see objects before you.
This truth will exert an influence on minds that cannot
be reached by principles.

Now take the moral import and apply it all through
society. You will not forget that there are many
heavenly eyes constantly watching your footsteps.
However faithless, however worthless, however fleet
you may travel on earth, you cannot get away from
them. Neither can you escape from yourself! Go
steal a gold watch or a treasure, be false and deceive
others, if you choose; you will never be able to get away
from yourself; nor can you hide away from those
"guardians" who love you, who know whatever you
do, and who are always seeking to save, and cherish,
and make you better. Carry this memory with you
through life. It is not the gospel of "fear." But it is
the doctrine of truth, which puts a strange and mysterious check on the play of ungoverned appetites and
passions. All intuitive souls naturally believe that the
over-arching heavens are "full of eyes." It was this
conviction which inspired the following very appropriate lines :—

> Ah me! the solemn thought that man
> Is compassed by such eyes as these!
> That every action from its birth
> A purer nature sees!

Perchance they mark not acts alone;
  It may be thoughts lie open, too:
Each sin committed and conceived,
  The sinless angels view.

Ah! what a sight for holy eyes,
  The open heart of sinful man!
What is their pity, what their grief,
  When such a sight they scan!

They see the good, whose head is crowned
  With praise from every human lip,
Full of all frailty when disguise
  From his weak heart they strip.

They mark how selfishness defiles
  The love which men esteem most pure:
They mark how oft the virtue slips
  We blindly hold most sure.

Well might we shudder at the gaze
  That sees what lies most deep within,
If angels loved, like men, to mark
  The weakness and the sin.

They love to succor and to heal;
  In woe they soothe, in guilt reprove:
It is for kindly offices
  They leave their home above.

CHAPTER XVII.

THE SUMMER LAND AS SEEN BY CLAIRVOYANCE.

I now behold the forms of earth and the bodies of men, including my own, in a light and with a degree of perception never before presented. I discover that I can only see the forms by judging what and where they are, by the light of the spirit: for the outer body is beyond my perception, and I only see well-constituted and living spirits. By possessing this perception, I am enabled to commune with all the possessions of this Sphere, and now behold the extended fields and living habitations of this elevated existence.

There are to be observed three specific degrees of form and development: the young and unmatured; the advanced stages of these up to the mediatorial degree of manhood; and the highest of them all, which is the perfect form and most highly developed of all the spirits there existing.

I perceive that whenever an *infant* dies on any of the earths, the undeveloped body of its spirit becomes deposited in this Sphere, and is fully unfolded in intellect, and highly enlightened concerning all of its own existence and prior situation. The infant that has had life and dies in infancy, is, I perceive, in this Sphere,

---

NOTE.—It may be a source of instruction and satisfaction to those who have not yet examined works on the Spiritual Philosophy, to read a few extracts from " Nature's Divine Revelations," pp. 647, *et seq.*

fully developed and perfected. So it is with all unin-
formed spirits who escape the body on any earth ; for
each is here educated in the truths and beauties of the
whole existence. So it is also with the intelligent and
highly cultivated ; for they are here more advanced,
and occupy a position more elevated and refined.

Moreover, I discover three distinct *societies* or associations of men and females, each occupying a position
determined by their degree of cultivation, sympathy for
one another, and power of approaching each other's
sphere of knowledge and attainment. And what is
well to relate is, that each society is encompassed by a
peculiar sphere or atmosphere, which is an exhalation
from the specific quality of their interior or spiritual
characters. Every spirit has a peculiar sphere of its
own, and also a general one in which it can with
pleasure exist. And spirits know and associate with
each other according to the quality of the sphere which
is exhaled from their interiors. They associate only
as spheres are agreeable, and as they are capable of
approaching each other with pleasure.

So it is also with mankind on earth. They dwell in
each other's society only as they can coalesce, and
approach each other with pleasure. So also are existing on earth the three specific degrees of development,
which are youth, manhood, and mature age. But they
are in a rudimental condition, and not situated in order
as they are in the Second Sphere.

I perceive that spirits approach other according to
the relative degrees of brilliancy which surrounds and
encompasses their forms. Thus association is determined and made perfect by the law of congeniality and

affinity, or affection. They have an affection for one another in proportion to the similarity in the degrees of love and purity to which they have attained. Thus are the three states or societies established.

In the *first* society are an immense number of infant and uncultivated spirits, which are in various degrees of advancement and cultivation, according as such have proceeded from the earth. In the *second* group or society are those who have become highly instructed in the principles and truths of the Divine Mind. And into this society all who die on earth with minds properly unfolded are immersed, because here they can associate agreeably. In the *third* society I discover spirits of the most enlightened character. The most of them proceed from the planets Jupiter and Saturn, and also from planets in other solar systems. This society is so highly illuminated with wisdom that it is almost impossible for the spirits of the lower societies to approach it. If they make an effort to enter their midst, this is immediately overcome by the strong repulsion arising from the non-affinity existing between them and their respective spheres.

The atmosphere that flows from and encompasses and protects the first society, is of a mingled and rather unilluminated appearance. Its brilliancy is rather faint in comparison to that of those above it. It appears gloomy, dark, and rather uncongenial, because it is an emanation from uncultivated intellects. Yet there is a purity—an exceeding purity among them, viewed comparatively with that existing on earth.

The *second* society is enveloped with an atmosphere of far more congenial variegations, presenting a resplendent brilliancy which indicates purity and elevation. It appears like the mingling of many colors, such as are not known on earth. And these are all so perfectly conjoined, and are blended together in such harmony, that the whole *aroma* is of itself a representation of purity and refinement. Yet it is a sphere emanating from the whole body of the society, indicating the wisdom of the spirits composing it. Their wisdom consists in a knowledge of truths and principles concerning material and rudimental things; and in them they are highly enlightened. And the inconceivable variety of colors surrounding them arises from their dissimilar stages of intellectual advancement. Yet they are all in the same plane of wisdom, and thus form one society, enveloped by this beautiful and refined atmosphere.

The *third* society is also clothed with an aërial garment, which is a perfect representation of the character and perfection of their interiors. I behold in it all colors, and a variety of reflections proceeding from the subordinate societies; and these reflections render their spiritual emanation so very beautiful that language is inadequate to describe it.

Those of the *first* society are in the plane of natural thought; that is, they are just emerging from the instructions and impressions of earth, into the wisdom of the higher societies.

The *second* society is in the plane or sphere of *causes;* that is, they are just emerging from a superior knowledge of visible effects presented on earth, to a perception of the interior causes of them : and their wisdom extends to the lowest and first cause of all material

things. Therefore they have a knowledge of all
interior causes, essences, and their modes of external
manifestation : but they are not in the possession of
superior wisdom concerning the *uses* for which causes
and effects were instituted.

The *third* society is in the plane of *effects ;* and
those composing it have a perception of all ultimate
design, and of the universal adaptation of things to
each other. Their minds are exceedingly luminous.
With their powers of penetration, the externals of
things are laid open, and they perceive only the character and quality of the interior. Their vision extends
to every recess of their own habitation, and their
knowledge comprehends all subordinate material existences. They have a most unlimited presentation of all
created things below their elevated position ; and their
wisdom is light, and love, and brilliancy, and even
ecstasy, to a degree that transcends description. With
their unfolded spiritual powers they behold the vast
landscapes of the spirit-home, too extensive to be comprehended by men on earth, and too beautiful to be
appreciated or enjoyed by them.

The *third* society are not only in a state of emerge-
ment from the plane of causes to that of effects, but
also from their sphere to the third world of human
existence.

And what is well to relate is, that notwithstanding
the dissimilitude that exists between the three societies,
there is a perfect unity among them, and a mutual
dependence one upon another ; and there is a continual
aspiring affection that gyrates from the infant intellect
to the high and superior wisdom of the third society.

There is a unity of action, an agreeableness of situation, and a propriety of position, which cause them all to live one for another, like a brotherhood.

And, moreover, it is profitable to remark that each society or group is well situated, well conditioned, and well cultivated, in reference to the specific state which each is compelled to sustain. The situations are perfect in proportion to the degree of wisdom and refinement to which each has attained. The lowest appears inferior in comparison to the higher and superior; though even the first, to man on earth, would appear to be a high state of perfection. By the varieties of condition and development, the societies are made perfect. They are thus as one brotherhood, joined by mutual affections and actions, and perpetuated in goodness by the benign and gentle influences that proceed from the highest society to the lower ones, and from these to it again.

The societies in the Second Sphere are very much to be admired, because of the perfect harmony which pervades them, and the perfect melody and concert of rudimental and perfected knowledge which they manifest. In a corresponding manner does there exist a concert of action, a unity of feeling, and a universal love, one for another.

The inhabitants do not converse *vocally*, but immerse their thoughts into one another by radiating them upon the countenance. And I perceive that thought enters the spirit by a process of *breathing*, or rather it is introduced by influx, according to the desires of those conversing. They perceive thought by and through the eyes, inasmuch as *these*, like the general countenance, are an index to the quality and workings of the interior. They seemingly *hear* each other converse; but that is owing to a previous knowledge of sound by which words are distinguished and their meaning apprehended.

They perceive things without them by their sense of *vision;* but they are conscious that it is the *reflection* which they perceive, and not the *substance.* Therefore, they exercise *judgment* concerning all they perceive— not judging from sensuous observation, but from the character of the substance observed.

I also discover that spirits in this Sphere approach and associate with each other according to the mutual affinity subsisting between them, even as do the inhabitants of earth; but the difference is in the *mode* of associating. Men on earth associate with one another by the guidance of their gross and rudimental senses, as these are productive of inclination and desire. Instead of this, men associate in this higher Sphere by a knowledge of each other's inherent purity, and the state of each other's affections.

Moreover, I perceive that the *former experience* of every person, both male and female, is treasured up in the memory, from which they can extract representations of that which they previously knew or experienced. Every thing appears indelibly impressed upon the memory, and is mirrored forth with a vividness in proportion to the strength of the impression. Therefore, whatever thought enters the human mind on earth, becomes a resident in the memory, and is here brought forth with the appearance of newness that makes it both interesting and instructive. Those things

experienced which are disagreeable to the memory are
deposited in its depths and concealed from the view of
any other being, by the prevalence of those events and
experiences which it pleases the mind to remember,
and which the mind takes delight in contemplating.
Hence it is proper for all men on earth to do and think
only that which pleases them most (according to wisdom), and which they would most earnestly desire to
remember; and *not* to do those things, or encourage
those thoughts, which are opposed to the superior
delights of the mind. If this cannot be done in the
present social and mental condition of the world, then
it is proper to *change* those conditions, so that even *this*
great good and pleasure may be obtained.

When spirits conversing appeal to each other's
memory, the memory mirrors forth a perfect representation of the thing remembered, which is perceived and
understood by the conversing spirit. I behold beautiful representations in the memory of those in the higher
societies. These representations are of the most exquisite character, because they proceed from the memory
of highly enlightened intellects; and they are therefore
delightful, inviting, and instructive.

I perceive that every thing in this Sphere is created
and manifested only by and through the exercise and
direction of *wisdom*. Hence the perfect order and
uniformity that subsist, and the inexpressible happiness
that flows as a consequence from such exquisite harmony and unity of action. Every thing is appreciated
as a blessing conferred upon them by the light and life
of Divine Love, and the order and form of Divine
Wisdom.

It is pleasing to behold these heavenly societies; for I see them at this moment existing in the most perfect degree of brotherly love, and joined inseparably together by constant ascending and descending affections. How very clear and bright are their countenances and expressions! They are unblemished by artificiality, and unspotted by rudimental and gross intrusions—for they are above and superior to these, and highly developed. The first society is indeed low, in comparison to the highest; but the variety and the degrees nevertheless form of the whole a complete brotherhood. The diversity consists in the different degrees of development; and the lowest cannot approach the highest, because of the dissimilarity of quality and spheres. But the lowest contains and involves the highest, while the latter, in return, comprehends and pervades the whole Sphere, manifesting a grace and beauty beyond the power of language to describe. And there exists almost an infinite variety of dispositions, of loves, of affections, and of wisdom, among them; yet each modification of previous conditions of mind is only an ascending degree of refinement toward perfection.

The whole is beautiful—surpassingly beautiful and sublime! for there exists that continual emanation of love and wisdom from societies and individual forms, displaying a brilliancy of illumination beyond any light or color on earth. It is even so very bright and beautiful, that those in the lower societies who approach are almost thrown into ectasies of delight. They become prostrated, and apparently fall on their faces, because of the beauty and brilliancy of the *aroma* that encompasses the superior societies of the spirit-home.

Thus it is that all preserve an order in their lives and situations; and thus it is that their approach to each other is graduated according to the unfolding of the spiritual senses and faculties to the external. They represent the circular and spiral forms; for there exists among them a uniform and also an ascending movement. And one is continually unfolding the possessions of another, even as from the germ are unfolded the body and the flower. And even as the flower perpetuates the species of the plant, so does the superior society pervade the lower ones, and is constantly introducing them into its own vast possessions; and thus all go onward to a still higher Sphere of spiritual and intellectual elevation.

9

CHAPTER XVIII.

SYNOPSIS OF THE IDEAS PRESENTED.

Coleridge's intellect must have been endowed with insight, for no poet ever more forcibly pictured the great truth of primordial developments :—

> " Contemplant Spirits! ye that hover o'er
> With untired gaze the immeasurable fount
> Ebullient with creative Deity !
> And ye of plastic power, that interfused
> Roll through the grosser and material mass
> In organizing surge !   Holies of God !"

The first goings forth or out-births from the great celestial Center are essential oceans of matter. These, after due elaboration or gestation, give birth to suns— and become cognizable to the outward senses of man. These suns become centers, or mothers, from which earths are born, with all the elements of matter, and each minutest particle infused with the vivifying, vitalizing spirit of the parent Formator. The Essences of heat or fire—electricity, etherium, magnetism—are all the natural or outward manifestations of the pro- ductive energy, the vitalizing Cause of all existences. It pervades all substances, and animates all forms.

The order of progression of solid matter is from the lower to the higher, from the crude to the refined, from the simple to the complicated, from the imperfect to the perfect—but in distinct degrees or congeries. That is, the lower must first be developed, to elaborate the materials and prepare the way for the higher. Thus, after the sun gave birth to the earth—and the same of all other planets—by the action of the vitality within the particles of matter, and its constant emanation in the form of heat, light, electricity, &c.—first from the great Central sphere to the sun, and thence to the earth, acting upon the granite and other rocks, with the atmosphere, the water, and other compound and simple elements—new compounds were formed, possessing the vital principle in sufficient quantities to give definite forms, as crystallization, organization, motion, life, sensation, intelligence—the last being the highest or ultimate attribute of production on our earth, and possessed or reached to perfection only by man.

A glance at the progress of matter in the production of our earth and its inhabitants, will serve as an illustration of the same process and progress of worlds in the vast expanse of the universe, that are perpetually and incessantly being brought into existence, and ultimating the grand object of the whole—namely, to develop and perfect individualized, self-conscious, ever-existing, immortal spirits, that shall be in the " image and likeness " of the Central Cause, and dwell forever in the Summer Spheres of space.

I now recapitulate the process of the earth's origin. Within the circumference of the sun, elementary particles of matter gather around a nucleus, which continues to aggregate and increase in dimension and variety of parts, in its perpetual and endless revolutions and evolutions, gradually advancing toward the outer surface of this fiery orb, as it increases in complexity and density, until it approaches the extreme verge of the sun ; when, by the impetus or centrifugal force it has attained, from its more compact structure and consequent increase of specific gravity, it breaks loose from its parent and flies off at a tangent into illimitable space. If a ball of lead and another of cotton of the same size be tied each to a string, and whirled violently around until the strings break, the lead ball will fly off in almost a straight line, for a long distance, before it makes a curve toward the earth; while the cotton ball will perform a graceful curve from the moment it breaks loose, and soon falls to the ground. The experiment will illustrate the movements of a planet, when, first thrown off from the sun (being much more dense); or, in other words, it will account for the eccentric movement of comets, which, in fact, are new-born and baby earths or planets. The extreme tenuity, fluidity, and rarefaction of its particles, and its consequent feeble cohesive attraction, and its irregular orbital and axillary movements, give the new earth elongated, attenuated, and many various forms, as presented to the beholder on another planet. Sometimes it happens that the caudal extremity gets so "long drawn out," and so far from the center of gravity—the proper polarity or axis not being yet fully established—that a part or parts become detached or broken off. The detached parts become meteoric bodies, or else " satellites," which continue to revolve around and within the orbit of the new earth. Our earth has one belt of these meteoric *parasites*. Other planets several.

In the lapse of ages, the attractive and repulsive, or

the centripetal and centrifugal forces become equalized, the particles of matter have formed more intimate associations, the outer surfaces have locked up a large portion of the free caloric within the embrace of their own substance, and have consequently condensed and hardened — a globular form has succeeded the oblate sphere, with its spinal extremity, and a *regular* orbit is defined and maintained. Oxygen and nitrogen have united in the proper proportions to form the atmosphere ; oxygen and hydrogen have combined to form water ; oxygen and silicon have entered into an adamantine embrace to form quartz rock ; oxygen and carbon have formed a tripartite union with calcium, producing immense beds of carboniferous lime-stone. Numerous other combinations of oxygen with gases, metals, and other elements—and these again combining with other simple or compound substances, have brought out of this vast amorphous mass of elementary materials, as they existed in an intensely heated and rarefied state, when first thrown off from the sun, new, and more solid, and more permanent forms.

In all this beautiful, harmonious, and ever-progressive plan of productive affinities, oxygen plays a very conspicuous part, as a positive, energizing, vitalizing principle, electricity, Galvanism, and magnetism being different developments of the *same* principle. It appears to have grasped and to have held fast within its embrace the very germs of vitality. Phosphorus is another form of its tangible development, not yet understood by chemists or physiologists. No living plant or animal can exist without it. It is always found in the seeds and germinal principles, and in the substances of the brain and nerves, but in no other part of vegetables or animals, as entering into an organic compound.

In the course of time, when "the waters had subsided," the heat and light emanating continually from the sun—upon the waters of the seas, and in rain, and mist, and dew—acted upon the surfaces of the granite and other rocks, abrading, decomposing, and uniting with their elements to produce other new compounds of a more refined and perfect nature. Thus, large beds of gelatinous matter were formed in shallow pools beneath the water level, and a slimy coating upon the surfaces of the rocks above the water. [See *Great Harmonia*, vol. 5, Part III.] Thus soil was first formed—a preparation, elaboration, and combination of material, susceptible of developing vegetable life, marine and terrestrial. The first vegetable forms springing from these slimy rocks were simple, and not defined in their structure, being lichens, or cryptogamous plants, about seventy per cent. of whose substance is gelatin.

As one forcible evidence of the fact of vegetables first originating from the elements of the rock on which they germinate, and from the heat, light, atmosphere, and moisture, is, that each rock of different chemical composition, when exposed to these influences, will produce a moss peculiar to itself, and the same rock, in any latitude where it can grow, will always produce a plant of the same species, and each plant in its turn, of the thousands. of classes, orders, genera, species, and varieties now in existence, will invariably produce an animalcule, or insect, peculiar to itself. These are facts that have been abundantly substantiated by the most scientific naturalists of the age.

The first forms of vegetation were brought into being, and perfected in their kind—elaborating from their own substance a germ or nucleus of vitality with the impress of its own individuality, inclosed within a receptacle capable of preserving and sustaining it, till the favorable action of the elements (in heat, light, moisture, and the soil) could bring forth from each germ or seed " an image and likeness " of its parent— the organized substance or body of the original plant, having performed the ultimate object of its existence, dies, and the elements of which it is composed mingle with the thin soil on the surface of the rocks, adding to its substance, increasing its complexity, and refining its particles ; so that, with the return of the vernal equinox, and the genial rays of the sun, not only the seeds of the old lichen unfold and expand into the same species, but a new and more complicated plant, with distinct and marked differences (perhaps a fern), makes its appearance, and rears its graceful stem, and spreads its glossy foliage above the lowly moss.

Thus the ever-present and ever-active principle of vitality and creative Energy, acting and reacting upon the materials of our globe, started the kingdoms of Nature, which have and will ever continue to progress —from the simple to the more complicated vegetable forms : animalculæ, infusia, radiata, mollusca, verte- brata, and Man as the Ultimate. The lowest and imperfect first, and the more complex and perfect after, in regular progression, but in distinct degrees. Each new type being dependent upon *all* that preceded it for its existence, but yet distinct and different from its predecessors.

Thus it requires certain conditions, proportions, and combinations of elementary inorganic substances to produce a vegetable—and vegetable growth is dependent entirely upon elementary regimen—while animals cannot be produced or sustained in their existence by inorganic or elementary matter. The organic compounds of the blood, muscular fiber, gelatin, skin, hair, nails, or horns, &c., are all formed in exact constituents or proportions from the elementary particles that enter into their composition from the vegetable. The vegetable kingdom must, therefore, have existed *before* the animal—the vegetable realm being the stepping-stone, or connecting-link, between the elementary or mineral kingdom and the animal. Hence, if the vegetable kingdom should by any cause be blotted out from the face of the earth, the animal would soon be annihilated.

Each type of the endless variety of inorganic and organized substances is but a link in the great chain of cause and effect, and each type or species is so marked and distinct as easily to be distinguished, and each variety and unity of the human species is so indelibly stamped with its own perfected individuality as to be recognized from the myriads of the same species.

Thus fixed, unvarying, and universal laws of the Father govern and regulate all his universe. Throughout all the ramifications of the spiritual, physical, and celestial, eternal unity, order, and harmony reigns—conception, development, progression, and perfection mark all things, and all point with irresistible force of reason and demonstration to the immortality of the Spirit.

In taking this philosophical view of the plan and progress of Nature and the works of God, how grand, how sublime, how comprehensive, how rational and satisfactory—to the independent-thinking and inquiring mind, who wishes to "have a reason for the faith that is within him "—how perfectly are the love and wisdom and justice of the Father and Mother conjugated and displayed! And how real, conclusive, and overwhelming the evidence—appealing directly to the senses, the intellect, and the affections—of the self-conscious, immortal existence and progressive happiness of the "spirit" that is within us! The human race being the last and highest development of earth, and mind the only organism possessing reason and intelligence that examines and investigates all that is beneath and around itself, and that has a consciousness of the future— endeavoring to raise or draw aside the thin, semi-transparent vail that hangs suspended between the physical and spiritual existence—analogy, "reasoning from what we know," points directly not only to the probability, but to the absolute *certainty and necessity* of a future existences called the Summer Land.

All organic forms below man not only produce their like, but the substance of their material forms mingle with previously formed compounds, to produce a new and *distinct type* superior to itself. *But the human type has no superior development*, and there is no retrogression in the works of Nature. Each new unfolding is superior to the preceding. Man, then, is destined for other and higher Spheres. In those Spheres, or new states of existence, man's spirit must present not only an "image and likeness" of Nature and God, but

9*

a consciousness of identity and individual selfhood. Feeling and knowing this, he should so live while in this rudimentary and preparatory state of existence, that all his physical, intellectual, moral, and spiritual structure, formation, growth, and maturity, be fully developed, cultivated, and perfected; so that when the "mortal puts on immortality," and seeks "a home in the heavens," it can expand into a celestial life, without spot or blemish to mar its beauty or impede its progress in bliss and glory eternal.

THE END.

JUST PUBLISHED.

A VOICE FROM THE INNER LIFE—A NEW WORK,

BY

ANDREW JACKSON DAVIS:

ENTITLED

ARABULA;

OR,

THE DIVINE GUEST.

This new volume, just published in first-rate style, is, to some extent, a sequel to the "MAGIC STAFF," the Author's Autobiography.

THE ARABULA

Is an entirely new work from the INTERIOR; being at once a biographical and a spiritual production. It is a volume of over 400 pages, and contains inspirations from the following new Saints: St. Rishis, St. Menu, St. Confucius, St. Siamer, St. Syrus, St. Gabriel, St. John, St. Pneuma, St. James, St. Gerrit, St. Theodore, St. Octavius, St. Samuel, St. Eliza, St. Emma, St. Ralph, St. Asaph, St. Mary, St. Selden, St. Lotta.

WILLIAM WHITE & CO.,

158 WASHINGTON STREET, BOSTON, MASS.

544 BROADWAY, NEW YORK.

LIST OF THE WORKS OF

ANDREW JACKSON DAVIS,

IN THE ORDER OF THEIR PUBLICATION.

Cost of the Complete Works of A. J. Davis.

Complete works of A. J. Davis, comprising twenty volumes, seventeen cloth, three in paper. Nature's Divine Revelations, 30th edition, just out. 5 vols., Great Harmonia, each complete—*Physician, Teacher, Seer, Reformer* and *Thinker.* Magic Staff, an Autobiography of the Author. Penetralia; Harbinger of Health, Answers to Ever-Recurring Questions, Morning Lectures (20 discourses), History and Philosophy of Evil, Philosophy of Spirit Intercourse, Philosophy of Special Providences, Harmonial Man, Free Thoughts Concerning Religion, Present Age and Inner Life, Approaching Crisis, Death and After Life, Children's Progressive Lyceum Manual, Arabula or Divine Guest, Stellar Key to the Summer Land—full set, $26, sent by mail or express as soon as ordered.

WILLIAM WHITE & CO.,

158 WASHINGTON STREET, BOSTON, MASS.,

544 BROADWAY, NEW YORK.

BANNER OF LIGHT:

A Journal of Romance, Literature, and General Intelligence ; also an Exponent of the Spiritual Philosophy of the Nineteenth Century.

PUBLISHED WEEKLY

AT No. 158 WASHINGTON STREET, BOSTON, MASS.
BRANCH OFFICE, 544 BROADWAY NEW YORK.

WILLIAM WHITE & CO., Proprietors.

WILLIAM WHITE.　　　　ISAAC B. RICH.　　　　CHARLES H. CROWELL.

LUTHER COLBY................Editor.
LEWIS B. WILSON, Assistant Editor.
AIDED BY A LARGE CORPS OF THE ABLEST WRITERS.

TERMS OF SUBSCRIPTION, IN ADVANCE:

Per Year $3.00
Six Months... 1.50
Single Copies...................................8 Cents.

☞ *There will be no deviation from the above prices.*
When drafts on Boston or New York cannot be procured, we desire our patrons to send, in lieu thereof, a Post-office money order.

Subscriptions discontinued at the expiration of the time paid for.

Subscribers in Canada will add to the terms of subscription 26 cents per year, for pre-payment of American postage.

POST-OFFICE ADDRESS.—It is *useless* for subscribers to write, unless they give their *Post-Office Address* and *name of State.*

Subscribers wishing the direction of their paper changed from one town to another, must always give the name of the *Town, County, and State* to which it has been sent.

☞ *Specimen copies sent free.*
Subscribers are informed that twenty-six numbers of the BANNER compose a volume. Thus we publish two volumes a year.

ADVERTISEMENTS inserted at twenty cents per line for the first, and fifteen cents per line for each subsequent insertion.

☞ All communications intended for publication, or in any way connected with the Editorial Department, should be addressed to the EDITOR. Letters to the Editor, not intended for publication, should be marked "private" on the envelope.

All Business Letters must be addressed:

"BANNER OF LIGHT, BOSTON, MASS."

WILLIAM WHITE & CO.

THE CHILDREN'S
PROGRESSIVE LYCEUM.
A MANUAL,

With directions for the Organization and Management of Sunday-Schools, adapted to the Bodies and Minds of the Young, and containing Rules, Methods, Exercises, Marches, Lessons, Questions and Answers, Invocations, Silver-Chain Recitations, Hymns and Songs.

Original and Selected.

By ANDREW JACKSON DAVIS.

> "A pebble in the streamlet scant
> Has changed the course of many a river;
> A dew-drop on the baby plant
> Has warped the giant oak forever."

☞ The Lyceum externally is a work of art—its emblems all bearing a beautiful meaning—every color having its own divine significance—every badge telling the story of its group, and every group indicating one step higher in progress. The pretty picturesque targets all point to the top of the mountain, "Liberty" farthest up the ascent, with the white badge fluttering wing-like upward, and beckoning to the little ones at the "Fountain" to gather up their ribbons (red, like the heart-glow of childhood), and follow to that pearly gate, where the angels wait to let them in. Religion is natural—this is one of its most natural expressions, leading to harmony, love, and happiness.

"Suffer little children to come unto me," said the gentle Nazarene, "for of such is the Kingdom of Heaven." Is it strange then that one lovely constellation of pure little ones should attract to us the holiest and most divine influences? If any doubt that this Lyceum movement is an *inspiration*, let them stand among the Groups a single day; let them feel the holy influences that fall in showers from the higher spheres, the uprisings of the soul, as involuntarily it answers to the call from its true home, the inspirations that fall upon the heart like angel breathings, thrilling each string with melody, and filling the whole being with a yearning for God and Heaven.

Price, per copy, 80 cents, and 8 cents postage if sent by mail; and for 100 copies, $63.00.

Address the Publisher,

BELA MARSH,

No. 14 BROMFIELD ST., BOSTON.

NEW PAPER FOR CHILDREN.

THE

LYCEUM BANNER.

PUBLISHED TWICE A MONTH,

BY

MRS. L. H. KIMBALL.

Edited by Mrs. H. F. M. Brown.

It is an OCTAVO, printed on good paper, and embellished with fine electrotype illustrations.

Some of our best writers are engaged as regular contributors.

We teach no human creeds: Nature is our law-giver; to deal justly our religion. The children want Amusement. History. Romance, Music—they want Moral, Mental, and Physical Culture. We hope to aid them in their search for these treasures.

And at the Fourth National Convention of Spiritualists, held at Cleveland, Ohio, September 3d, 4th, 5th, and 6th, 1867, it was

"*Resolved*, That this Convention recognize the permanency and force of early religious impressions, and the importance of keeping the minds of our children and youth untrammeled by theological tenets, and that we do earnestly recommend to the Spiritualists of America the institution known as the Children's Progressive Lyceum, and ask them to sustain it by their sympathy and means until the development of our philosophy shall enable us to secure a more efficient means of education."

At the same Convention, the following preamble and resolutions were adopted:

"*Whereas*, The Lyceum interests are of such vast importance in the work of progress; and

"*Whereas*, An interchange of views with regard to the management and various exercises connected with this great educational movement: therefore.

"*Resolved*, That the Convention recommend the establishment of a Lyceum Statistical Bureau, for the purpose of interchanging thoughts relative to this work, and that we recommend the

"LYCEUM BANNER AS THE ORGAN OF THAT BUREAU."

TERMS OF SUBSCRIPTION.

One Copy, one year, *in advance*		$1.00
Ten Copies, to one address		9.00
Twenty-five Copies, "		22.50
Fifty Copies. "		45.00
One hundred Copies, "		90.00

Address,

Mrs. LOU H. KIMBALL,

P. O. Drawer 5956, Chicago, Ill.

Fourth Abridged Edition

OF THE

Children's Lyceum Manual,

BY

ANDREW JACKSON DAVIS.

———•◆•◆•◆•———

JUST published, a beautiful, compact, yet comprehensive little volume, containing all necessary instructions for

CHILDREN'S PROGRESSIVE LYCEUMS.

These attractive institutions, known as Spiritualistic Sunday-Schools, have multiplied rapidly during the past year. Adults as well as children seem to take equal interest in the proceedings of these Lyceums.

In this Manual will be found *Rules, Marches, Lessons, Invocations, Silver Chain Recitations, Hymns* and *Songs.* Spiritualists, and Friends of Progress generally, can now take immediate steps in behalf of the true *Physical* and *Spiritual education of their Children,* at about one-half the price of the unabridged edition.

The above work is comprised in a volume of 158 pages, 32mo. It is printed on good paper, and neatly bound in cloth.

Price, per copy, 44 cents, and 4 cents postage if sent by mail; for 12 copies, $4.56; and for 100 copies, $34.

Address the Publisher,

BELA MARSH,

No. 14 Bromfield Street, Boston.

DEPOT FOR LYCEUM EQUIPMENTS.
E. WATERS & SONS,
No. 303 River Street, Troy, N. Y.

A CHILDREN'S PROGRESSIVE LYCEUM, when fully organized, in accordance with the recently developed system, requires the following equipments :—

TWELVE TARGETS, with title and number of group, and age of the members, beautifully printed on each side, with *twelve small silk flags* (10x15) for each target below the staff, mounted, ready for use. Each target corresponds in *color* to the color of the badges worn by the members of the group. These targets are firmly fixed in staffs five feet and four inches long, with a joint in the center; a brad in the lower end to fasten in the floor, and worsted galloon strings to tie the staff to the top of a chair or settee in the hall. We put in the strings so that they may be fastened to the staffs at the proper height. (For instructions, significations, &c., see the "Manual.")

TWELVE DOZEN PRINTED COTTON FLAGS, Stars and Stripes, of three different sizes, to suit different ages of the children. The smallest flags on red staffs, three feet long ; the next size on blue staffs, three feet six inches long ; the largest on black walnut—stained—four feet long, carried by the higher groups.

TWELVE SILK FLAGS (20x30), for Leaders. These beautiful flags are fastened on black walnut staffs, four feet nine inches long. The Leaders should carry handsomely mounted banners to distinguish them when marching.

ONE LARGE SILK FLAG (36x54), for the Guardian of the groups, on a staff six feet long, surmounted with an appropriate ornament.

TWELVE BADGES, appropriate for principal officers and their assistants, arranged in a strong paper box, properly labeled.

TWELVE DOZEN SILK BADGES, in durable labeled boxes, for leaders and members of the groups, in different colors, and differently ornamented. (For methods, meaning, &c., see the "Manual.")

CONDUCTOR'S BATON, black walnut stained, handsomely mounted with gilt ornaments.

TICKETS OF MEMBERSHIP, handsomely printed in two colors, one ticket for each member.

A LYCEUM MANUAL (the abridged edition), for each officer, leader, and member, so that all may participate in the beautiful Songs, Hymns, Silver-Chain Recitations, &c.

A GUARDIAN'S JOURNAL, properly ruled and classified according to groups, and well bound.

GROUP BOOKS, for Leaders, one dozen in different colors, and properly ruled.

REWARDS OF MERIT, of several varieties, furnished at short notice.

BOOKS OF MS. MUSIC, for all the songs in Manual.

A BANNER CHEST, with tray for badges and manuals, is indispensable—five feet and two inches long and eighteen inches square, inside measure ; with lid to open back and level, supported by slides, to serve as a table on which to arrange the flags. This chest is furnished with a good lock and two or three keys—one for Conductor and one for each of the Guards.

And finally. A LIBRARY of valuable and entertaining books, free from sectarianism, adapted to children and young people generally. (The residents of every community have books appropriate to such a library, which they will doubtless freely contribute, if kindly invited to do so.)

☞ The undersigned will be happy to respond by letter and circular to questions relative to the organization and government of these attractive schools.

☞ The foregoing list of equipments (whole or in part), with the exception of books for the library, may be obtained at the most reasonable prices, by addressing

E. WATERS & SONS,
303 River St., Troy, N. Y.

PROSPECTUS

der

von dem amerikanischen Seher und Verkündiger der
"Harmonischen Philosophie"

ANDREW JACKSON DAVIS

in der

Reihenfolge ihrer Veröffentlichung in Nord-Amerika erschienenen und
mit Autorisation ihres Verfassers

eines Theils von

dem im Jahre 1858 verstorbenen

Präsidenten der Kaiserlich Leopoldinisch-Carolinischen Akademie der
Naturforscher zu Breslau,

Professor Dr. Christian Gottfried Nees von Esenbeck,

und andern Theils von

dessen Mitarbeiter und Herausgeber

Gregor Constantin Wittig,

aus dem Englischen in's Deutsche übersetzten Werke.

———

These volumes, as fast as translated into the German language, will be
forwarded to America, and can be obtained at the offices of

WILLIAM WHITE & CO.,

158 WASHINGTON STREET, BOSTON, MASS., OR,

544 BROADWAY, NEW YORK.

NOW READY AND FOR SALE.

THE HARMONIA, 4th vol., *" THE REFORMER."*

ALSO

THE MAGIC STAFF, an Autobiography.

Price of each, $2.75. Postage, 32 cts.

www.ingramcontent.com/pod-product-compliance
Lightning Source LLC
Chambersburg PA
CBHW020611030726

47497CB00007B/2184

*9 7 8 3 3 3 7 3 7 2 5 8 3 *